William and the Masked Ranger

William and the Masked Ranger

Richmal Crompton

First published in 1966 by George Newnes Ltd., London.
First published 1973 in Armada by
William Collins Sons & Co. Ltd., 14 St. James's Place,
London S.W.1.

© Richmal Crompton Lamburn 1966

Printed in Great Britain by
Love & Malcomson Ltd., Brighton Road,
Redhill, Surrey.

CHAPTER I

WILLIAM AND THE MASKED RANGER

"So my whole life's got to be *ruined*," said William, flinging out his arms dramatically, "jus' cause of one dotty ole woman."

"Don't talk such nonsense, William," said Mrs. Brown. "Your life won't be ruined and Aunt Felicia isn't dotty. You've seen Western films and you'll probably see them again."

"But not this one," said William. "Not *The Masked Ranger*. It's not jus' an ordin'ry Western. It's blood-curdlin' an' nerve-shatterin'. It says so outside the cinema. There's a witch doctor in it that can put *real* spells on people an' an Indian that's got a secret plant that winds round people an' strangles them to death an' a white man that——"

"William, it sounds horrible," said Mrs. Brown with a shudder.

"But that's what it's *meant* to be," said William in exasperation. "Victor Jameson's seen it in London an' he says it's *fab*. It curdled his blood an' shattered his nerves all right. An' Ginger an' Henry an' Douglas are goin' to see it on Sat'day an' not me. Gosh! I'll be the only person in the whole place that won't have had their blood curdled an' their nerves shattered over it. There's a lion in it an' you axshully *see* it maulin' its victim an' you see an Indian axshully scalpin' a man an'——"

"Listen, William——" Mrs. Brown tried to interrupt,

but William was launched on his sea of eloquence and far beyond her reach.

"An' it's part of education, isn't it? It's part of education to learn about foreign places an' what they look like an' how people act in 'em. It's education, isn't it? I bet I'd learn a lot about this foreign place in this film an' it'd be good for my education. Well, you *want* me to be educated, don't you? I bet if I went to this film an' learnt about this foreign place an' about the people in it I might get a better report nex' term." He gave his ironic snort. "Seems funny to me that you want me to grow up uneducated jus' 'cause of this dotty ole woman."

"She's not dotty, William. She's very nice. You've not seen her since you were a baby."

"No, an' I don't want to," said William. "I don't want to see a person that's ruined my whole life. I——"

"That's enough, William. It's no use going on and on about it. It's just one of those things that can't be helped."

It was one of those things that couldn't be helped.

A girlhood's friend of Mrs. Brown's (whom William had not seen since babyhood but whom he knew as Aunt Felicia and from whom he received yearly birthday presents) had come to spend a holiday at an hotel in Marleigh and had invited Mrs. Brown and William to lunch and tea on the following Saturday. William had accepted the situation without enthusiasm but with only formal protests. And then the film, *The Masked Ranger*, had come to Hadley Cinema and William, Henry, Ginger and Douglas had planned to go to see it on the Saturday afternoon, taking Mrs. Brown's consent for granted. To their horror and surprise Mrs. Brown firmly refused to allow William to withdraw from the arrangement with Aunt Felicia.

"It's a prior engagement, William," she said.

"I don't care what it is " said William. "I think it's jus' tyranny, same as in hist'ry. It's same as sellin' people for slaves. I might as well *be* a slave, dragged off to that ole place at Marleigh when I might be seein' a blood-curdlin' an' nerv-shatterin' film that people'll probably be talkin' about for the rest of my life an' I'll be the only person in the whole world that's not seen it."

"But William, you can't break one engagement just because another more attractive one has come along after you've accepted it. You must learn to behave like a civilised human being."

"I don't *want* to behave like a civilised. yuman bein'," said William. "I'd rather be a savage any day. I bet they don't let themselves be dragged off to dotty ole women when they'd rather go to see blood-curdlin' an' nerve-shatterin' Westerns."

"William, don't talk such nonsense. I keep telling you there'll be other Westerns coming to the cinema."

"Yes, if I live to see 'em," said William darkly. "I may not have long to live for all you know."

Mrs. Brown sighed wearily.

"William, do *please* go out and play with someone."

William remembered that Ginger, Henry and Douglas would be waiting for him at the old barn.

"All right," he said. He turned to her as he reached the door. "An' I hope you won't regret it when it's too late."

He trailed across the fields, his hands dug into his pockets, his toes dragging along the ground, his brows set in their most ferocious scowl.

"Ruined!" he muttered. "My whole life ruined! An' they jus' don't care."

His mind slid away to one of the day-dreams that often brought him solace in his conflicts with authority.

He succumbed to some swift and fatal disease, leaving his parents with only the memory of his short and beautiful life, and racked by remorse for not having let him see *The Masked Ranger*.

Somehow it failed to bring its usual glow of comfort and he turned to another of his favourite day-dreams. Suddenly (by what means he never could determine) he leapt to the loftiest pinnacle of fame, acclaimed and honoured by the highest in the land. His parents stood humbly in awe of him, but he was gracious and affable. He forgave them for their harsh treatment. "It's all right," he said when they apologized abjectly for not allowing him to see *The Masked Ranger*. "Don't give it another thought. It was a little hard on me but don't worry about it any more." He threw out his arms in an expansive gesture. "I'll take you both to a party at Buckingham Palace tomorrow an' I'll take you for a voyage round the world nex' summer holidays."

His lips were still curved in a smile of kindly condescesion when he joined Ginger, Henry and Douglas in the old barn.

"Well, is it all right?" said Ginger. "You'll be able to come with us on Sat'day, won't you?"

The smile of kindly condescension faded from William's lips, and his grievances closed over him again.

"No, she won't let me. Jus' 'cause we'd fixed up to go and see a dotty ole woman. Talked about civilised yuman bein's an' wouldn't listen to a word I said. I might have been a *worm*, the way she treated me." He shrugged. "Oh, well, let's go out an' do somethin'."

But it had begun to rain—a fine drizzle that increased to a steady downpour as they stood in the doorway watching it.

8

"Everythin' in the whole world seems to've turned against me," said William. "Even nature."

"There's goin' to be some good films at school nex' week," said Douglas, trying to lighten the atmosphere of gloom.

"Yes," said William bitterly. "All education an' stuff. Archaeology an' such like."

"Archaeology's jolly int'resting," said Henry.

"Not like a Western," said William. He gave his ironic snort again. "You can't get plots an' crimes an' villains in archaeology."

"Yes, you can," said Henry. "My father had a book out of the library an' I read some of it. There was an archaeological villain in it an' he did a plot an' a crime all right."

Reluctantly William dragged his mind from his own immediate problem.

"What did he do?" he said.

"He painted modern bones an' skulls to make 'em look like a prehistoric skeleton an' buried them an' then pretended to find them an' everyone thought it was a real prehistoric skeleton he'd found an' called it after him an' it made him famous all over the world. It was at a place called Piltdown. This book was all about it."

"Why did he do it?" said William, interested despite himself.

"No one quite knows," said Henry, "but they think it was because he thought that people didn't appreciate him."

"Treated him like a worm," said William with a return of bitterness.

"Yes . . . an' he thought he'd get even with them this way. He thought that when they did find out they'd look jolly silly bein' taken in by him an' he did it jolly cleverly

9

—it deceived experts—an' I 'spect he had a good laugh at them."

"Seems a funny sort of thing to do," said Ginger.

"No, I've read stories about that kind of crim'nal," said Henry earnestly. "Crim'nals that want to get their vengeance on Society for some intolerable wrong."

Douglas shook his head sadly.

"It was cheatin'," he said.

"I think he meant to tell them when he'd had a good laugh at them," said Henry, "but he died first. Anyway it made him famous an' it made all the others look silly when they found out. It was a jolly clever trick, really."

"I bet I could do it jus' as well," said William, adding thoughtfully, "I've a good mind to have a shot at it, too."

"You couldn't," said Ginger. "You don't know what a prehistoric skeleton looks like an' you haven't any bones."

"No," said William, "but I bet I could get some."

"You couldn't stick 'em together to make it look like a real skeleton," said Henry. "Not one that would deceive experts, anyway."

"P'r'aps not," admitted William, "but I could try somethin' else."

"What?" said Ginger.

"Look! It's stopped rainin'," said Douglas.

It had stopped raining. The clouds were clearing from a pale-blue sky.

"Come on," said Ginger. "Let's go'n' watch them fellin' those trees in Crown Wood. We might get some good sticks for arrows."

"All right," said William indifferently. His grievances had returned to him in full flood. "It doesn't seem to matter much what I do with my life now."

They crossed the field to the stile that led to the road. Victor Jameson was walking down the road.

"Hello," he said. "Goin' to *The Masked Ranger* on Saturday?"

"Not me," growled William.

"Why not?"

"Huh!" snorted William. "Funny sort of reason. 'Cause my parents don't care whether I get educated or not."

"Gosh! That's pretty hard on you," said Victor sympathetically. "It's a *fabulous* film! There's a part where this masked ranger an' an Indian baddy have a fight an' fall into a well together an' go on fightin' inside this well an'——"

"Oh shut up!" said William.

Victor was a friend of the Outlaws and his sympathy was genuine but there are times when even the sympathy of a friend is galling.

They walked on to the village and stood outside the post office window. There was the usual display of miniature cars massed between a pile of saucepans and a gardening trug brimming over with plimsolls.

"Nothin' new," commented Ginger.

"There wouldn't be," said William gloomily, "an' we haven't any money to buy it with even if there was."

"Good morning, boys."

Miss Radbury came briskly out of the post office, carrying her shopping bag. Miss Radbury lived at Rose Cottage. She was a retired don who occupied her retirement by writing historical biographies that were well received by critics and readers alike.

"G' mornin'," said the Outlaws, then turned their attention again to the display of miniature cars.

"I b'lieve that Daimler's new," said Ginger.

"No, it's not," said William. "It was there las' week."

Mrs. Monks came along the road, carrying a couple of library books under her arm. She stood talking with Miss Radbury at the door of the post office.

"Oh, I see you've been reading *The Kennystone Family*," said Miss Radbury, looking at the library books. "It's delightful, isn't it? Of course the author had the most incredible luck. She discovered a hoard of family letters and all she had to do was to weld them together. Nearly all the members had a finger in politics and one sees, as it were, the great events of history mirrored in the ordinary day-by-day life of the family." She laughed. "I wish I could have a stroke of luck like that."

They walked on down the road.

William turned to the others. His face was alight with the dawning of an Idea.

"Gosh!" he said. *"That's* what I could do."

"What?" said Ginger.

"Do a letter trick, same as that skeleton trick, to pay 'em out an' make 'em look silly."

"But how?" said Henry.

"Gosh! Don't you *see!*" said William. "I could sort of forge old letters from old families for someone to find an' write a book about."

"How could you forge old letters?" said Ginger.

"Write letters with bits of hist'ry in 'em an' put old dates at the top, like January the third 1500 or somethin' like that. Then they'd think they were old letters an' make a book about 'em. I bet I could do it as well as that skeleton man." His gloom had left him. His face wore a look of determination. "I'm jolly well goin' to have a try anyway."

"You couldn't, you know, William," said Henry, as they turned from the post office to walk slowly on through

12

the village. "They could tell they weren't real. They could see that the paper an' stamps weren't old."

"An' the writin'," said Ginger. "Old writin's got a special sort of look. A sort of *brown* look."

"Oh, I see you've been reading 'The Kennystone Family'," said Miss Radbury.

"I could use brown paint," said William, but he spoke without conviction. Gloom was closing over him again.

"Hello, boys!"

Miss Thompson hailed them from the garden of her cottage. She looked, as ever, kindly and vague and a little harassed.

"I've just taken some gingerbreads out of the oven,"

she said. "I think they'll be cool enough to eat. Would you like to come in and try them?"

They agreed eagerly. Even William's spirits rose. Miss Thompson was an excellent cook, but was apt to cook larger quantities than were required for a household of one. The Outlaws were frequently called in to dispose of the surplus.

They stood round the kitchen table, munching gingerbreads.

"I'm going away tomorrow," said Miss Thompson, "so I don't want to have any food left over. Really I don't know why I made them. I think it was because I was feeling worried and whenever I feel worried I start cooking. I find it soothes my nerves."

"I'm sorry you're worried, Miss Thompson," said Henry politely. "Is there anything we can do to help?"

"Thank you, dear, but I don't think there is," said Miss Thompson. "It's about some letters . . ."

"Letters?" said William indistinctly through a mouthful of gingerbread.

"Yes, dear. An aunt of mine had a sort of collection of family letters and she died a short time ago—I didn't know her well and I didn't like her much, so I can't pretend to be unduly distressed—and her companion has sent all these letters on to me. I don't find them of the slightest interest and I don't want to hoard the wretched things—I have enough things of my own to hoard—so I decided to burn them. The gardener was to have come today and made a garden fire but he can't come and it's too wet for a garden fire anyway. I could put them in the dustbin, of course, but it seems rather disrespectful to the dead to do that, don't you think? Burning seems so much more fitting somehow. And I do want to get them disposed of and off my mind before I go away."

14

The Outlaws were gazing at her open-mouthed.

"L-letters?" said William again.

"We've got an incinerator," said Ginger. "It burns things up jolly easily."

"How nice, dear," said Miss Thompson. "I mean to get one when my ship comes in."

Eagerly they set to work.

"We—we can take these letters an'—an' dispose of them for you," said William hoarsely.

"That *is* good of you," said Miss Thompson. "Now I can go away with a clear mind—my letters and gingerbreads safely disposed of. Thank you so much, boys. I'll just fetch the letters."

She went from the kitchen and returned a few moments later with an old-fashioned leather bag.

"They're all in there," she said, handing the bag to William. "I shall be so glad to get rid of them. Hoarding's such a *fatal* habit, don't you think?"

But the Outlaws were already outside the gate and making their way quickly down the road.

They sat on the floor in William's bedroom with the leather bag in the centre. Slowly, ceremoniously, William opened it and turned it upside down. Envelopes, yellowed by age, with old-fashioned writing and Victorian or Edwardian stamps, cascaded on to the carpet.

"Gosh!" said William. "Jus' look at 'em! Old envelopes an' old stamps an' everythin'! Come on! Let's open them an' see what's inside."

Eagerly they set to work, taking each letter out of its envelope, reading it, replacing it . . .

"The children have got measels."

"The Vicar's been to tea."

"The butcher's charged them too much."

"They've got black fly on the broad beans."

"They've got a new housemaid called Nelly."

"The curate preached too long."

"It's one of their birthdays and they've all joined together to buy him a camera."

"They went for a picnic and it rained."

"The dressmakers' made somethin' too tight an' it's got to be let out."

"The piano tuner's been."

"The Vicar's been to tea again."

"There isn't any hist'ry in them at all," said William disgustedly.

"Certainly it doesn't mirror anything very int'restin' in their day-by-day lives," said Henry.

"Jus' a waste of time goin' on readin' them," said Ginger.

"I told you it was wrong," said Douglas with gloomy triumph.

"Well, I'm not goin' to have taken all that trouble for nothin'," said William firmly. "*Tell* you what!" The light of an Idea gleamed again in his face "If there isn't any hist'ry in 'em let's *put* a bit of hist'ry in 'em."

"How?" said Henry.

"Easy as easy," said William. "Have you got pens or pencils?"

It turned out that each had a pen or pencil in his pocket.

"Come on, then," said William in a brisk, business-like voice.

He opened an envelope, took out the letter and scrawled across the bottom of the last sheet; "P.S. Someone told me there's a battle going on at Trafalgar. I wonder whose going to win. Nelson's got a wound in his eye and can't see signals."

"That's a good idea," said Ginger, impressed.

"Yes," said William. "We'll put a bit of hist'ry in all of them an' that'll make it a hist'ry mirror in day-by-day life all right."

They set to work with energy.

An account of a Church Bazaar ended with the words: "P.S. Christopher Colombus has jus' set off to discover America. I hope he gets there all right."

An account of the local Point-to-Point ended with the words: "P.S. I saw in the paper this morning that Charles the First has been executed. We'll have to wait till 1660 for the restoration."

Henry, whose energies were chiefly taken up in supervising the spelling of the other three, tried to confine his historical references within certain roughly defined limits. "Mr. Bell's just invented the telephone. We're going to have one put in next week." . . . "Queen Victoria went up in one of the new balloons this morning . They wanted to reach outer space but the gas began to leak and they had to make a forced landing." . . . "The Black Hole of Calcutta took place yesterday and tomorrow the six hundred are going to ride into the Valley of Death."

William's references spanned the whole field of history with wild abandon. "Henry VIII got married to the third of his six wives this morning." . . . "I went down to Hastings yesterday to watch the battle. Harold looked as if he'd got an arrow in his eye." . . . "I helped Guy Fawkes carry gunpowder into the House of Commons last night. We nearly got caught by a policeman." . . . "The civil war broke out yesterday. I'm going to enlist in the roundheads." . . . "I went to London in a horse-coach last week. It took hours and hours. I shall be jolly glad when someone invents railways." . . . "I was helping to put out the fire of London all yesterday. I feel rotten this morning. I think I must have caught the plague."

Douglas confined himself to the only historical film he had seen: "Someone told me this morning that Richard the Third was thinking of getting the princes murdered in the Tower if he could find a good murderer. He's swopped his kingdom for a horse and got into a muddle."

Ginger who had recently read a book called *Scenes from English History*, gave a brief account of his experiences in the Crusades (which included the Battle of Agincourt) and of his expedition to Canterbury with a band of pilgrims, led by Thomas à Becket.

"I'm gettin' a bit tired of this," said William at last, "an' I've used up all the hist'ry I know, anyway. We needn't put hist'ry in *all* of 'em. We've done enough to make it a jolly hist'ry mirror of day-by-day life. Come on. Let's pack 'em up in somethin' an' bury them."

"Where?" said Ginger.

"Anywhere," said William, then, "Tell you what! We'll bury it in Miss Radbury's garden then she can find it an' start writin' this book. It'll be a stroke of luck for her all right. We won't keep 'em in this bag 'cause the rain might get in. We'll find an old biscuit tin an' put 'em in that an' bury 'em. Come on."

They found an old biscuit tin, put the letters into it, and made their way to Miss Radbury's cottage. Notes pinned on the back door addressed to baker and milkman showed that Miss Radbury was out for the day. They surveyed the back garden. Since her retirement Miss Radbury had become an enthusiastic gardener. The vegetable patch was half dug over. The other half was rough and weed-infested.

"We'll put it in the part she's not dug," said William. "She'll start diggin' when she comes back an' find the tin an' then she can start writin' this book straight away."

Taking the spade that stood in the ground at the point where the digging had ceased, he eased the soil away from beneath a clump of towering weeds and slipped the tin into the hole, pushing the soil down over it.

"Now all she's got to do," he said, "is to write this book an' when it's famous all over the world we'll say we put the hist'ry in an' that'll make *us* famous all over the world an' they'll look jolly silly." He spoke a little uncertainly. The whole thing seemed more complicated than it had seemed when he first suggested it. "Oh, well," he continued briskly. "Let's go home now. We can't hang round here with her comin' back any minute. We'll come along tomorrow mornin' an' see what's happened."

They came the next morning and stood—a rather nervous-looking group—at the gate of Rose Cottage. No one seemed to be about. Cautiously, in single file, led by William, they made their way round to the vegetable patch at the back. The spade stood where it had stood the day before, but the clump of tall weeds had been moved and the box had gone.

"Gosh!" said William. "She's taken it."

"I 'spect she's started the book by now," said Ginger.

"She may have finished it," said Douglas. "Let's go down to the book shop in Hadley an' see if it's there."

"Don't be such a clot," said Henry. "It takes *weeks* to write a book."

The window of the room that overlooked the back garden was flung up and Miss Radbury's face appeared. It wore a friendly smile.

"Well, boys," she said, "have you come to make yourselves useful?"

They stared at her.

"I've got plenty of odd jobs for you in the garden," she went on, "if that's what you've come for. Wait a moment. I'll fit you out with tools."

She vanished and reappeared a few moments later with a gardening basket.

"You'll find all you want in here," she said. "Trowels and forks and gardening scissors. Now I'd like you to weed that border beneath the window. Take out the weeds, fork over the soil and cut off the dead heads of the flowers. I'll pay you Union wages for it. I've had a stroke of luck today." She laughed and disappeared round the side of the cottage.

The Outlaws laid down forks and trowels and gaped at each other.

Dazed and bewildered, taking the line of least resistance, the Outlaws settled down to weed the border, working on the general principle that the large growths were plants and the smaller ones weeds. From inside the window they could hear Miss Radbury telephoning a friend.

"Yes, the most marvellous find. . . . In a *tin* in the garden. . . . Yes, *buried*, . . . Would you believe it? . . . I went out to do a little digging in the garden last night and there it was. . . . I've no idea where it came from. Just a gift from the gods. . . . I must get on with my work now. I'll tell you all about it when I see you."

The Outlaws laid down forks and trowels and gaped at each other. Events were moving so swiftly that it was difficult to keep pace with them. William craned his neck to look cautiously through the window. Miss Radbury sat at a desk, writing. Her head was bent over her work. Her pen seemed to fly over the paper. William crouched down again.

"She's writin' the book," he said. His voice sounded faint and far-away. "Gosh! We've *done* it."

"Well, what happens now," said Douglas. "What do we do next?"

"Nothin'," said William. "It'll jus' get made into a book an' then they'll find out it's a trick an'—an' they'll look jolly silly."

They considered this in silence, while William pulled up a couple of calendulas and Ginger absent-mindedly loosened the soil round a luxuriant clump of dandelions.

Suddenly Miss Radbury appeared again round the corner of the cottage. She stood for a moment or two, inspecting the border.

"Oh dear!" she said. "You've pulled up my calendulas. Never mind. Just put them back. They'll come to no harm. . . . Now I won't keep you any longer. It's a lovely day and I'm sure you want to be off somewhere on your own devices. I'll pay you handsomely. I'm in a good mood because I've just had a wonderful find." She took out her purse and gave a half-crown to each of them. "Now put the basket and tools back into the shed and take yourselves off. I'm very busy this morning."

"Thanks *awfully* . . ."

She vanished again, and they saw her settle down again at her desk and continue writing.

"She's gettin' on quick with the book," said Ginger.

"Gosh! Half a crown!" said William.

In silence they replanted the calendulas, put basket and tools into the shed and made their way down to the gate. There they stood looking back at the cottage. They had achieved their purpose, they should have felt exhilarated and triumphant, but somehow they didn't. There was a curious feeling of flatness in the situation, together with an undercurrent of apprehension as if they had set in motion forces that they might not be able to control.

"I expect she'll get it finished by tonight," said William. "She's workin' jolly hard."

"But *she'll* be the one that'll look silly," said Ginger, "an' we didn't mean that."

"Yes, it's somehow got fixed on the wrong person," said Henry.

"Anyway," said William, pointing out the one redeeming feature of the situation. "It was a jolly clever trick an' it's come off."

"She's always been decent to us," said Ginger.

"Y-yes," agreed William. "Half a crown! An' she was decent about those calendars."

"Calendulas," said Henry.

"Well, whatever they are, she was decent about them."

23

"An' all we've done back is to make her look silly," said Ginger.

"I said it was wrong from the beginning," said Douglas.

"Well, we can't do anything about it now," said Henry. "What's done cannot be undone."

"Yes, it can," said William. His face was tensed in sudden resolve. "We can *get* it undone. We can go in an' tell her it was jus' a trick. Come on!"

He marched up to the open front door followed by the others, and beat a tattoo upon the knocker.

"Come in," called Miss Radbury.

They made their way in to the little study. Miss Radbury turned from her writing-table. She was still smiling amiably.

"Well, well, well," she said. "What is it now?"

"It's about this 'find' you found," said William gruffly.

"It was his vengeance on Society," said Henry, "for an intolerable wrong."

"He's never even seen this aunt," said Ginger.

"And she isn't even a real one," said Douglas.

"He might never get another chance of seein' *The Masked Ranger* all the rest of his life," said Henry.

"I've no idea what you're talking about," said Miss Radbury.

"The tin . . ." said William.

"The 'find' . . ." said Ginger.

Enlightenment shone through Miss Radbury's bewilderment.

"Oh, that . . ." she said. "I suppose you heard me telephoning and felt a bit curious about it. I'm always consumed by curiosity myself when I hear odd bits and pieces of conversation on the telephone. Well, I'll explain. Do any of you collect stamps?"

"No," said William.

24

"I do, you know. I've got a rather good collection, but the great gap in it was a certain Penny Black . . . Then, last night, I found a mysterious tinful of letters and on one of them was the Penny Black I wanted. I've no idea where the letters came from. I only read one or two of them, but one mentioned a Miss Thompson who seemed to live in this neighbourhood, so Miss Thompson may be able to unravel the mystery. She's away at present but I'll get into touch with her when she returns. If they are her property, of course, I'll pay her the market value of the Penny Black."

"She can buy an incinerator," said Douglas.

"The l-letters . . ." said William. The world seemed to be spinning round him. "The l-letters. . . . Was there any—any hist'ry in them?"

"History?" said Miss Radbury, puzzled. "Oh, I see what you mean. No, no reference at all to any historical events. All about church bazaars and new carpets and lantern lectures on Palestine and things like that. I only read one or two but it was enough. A thoroughly dreary family. Not down my street at all. But I'm thrilled by the Penny Black."

"Oh," said William.

The world was still spinning round him but a little less violently.

"And now," said Miss Radbury, "if I've satisfied your curiosity I'm afraid I shall have to ask you to run away. I'm writing a review on Professor Winterton's new book and I want to get it finished as quickly as possible. Good-bye for the present."

The Outlaws stammered their farewells and, as if in a dream, went out of the cottage and down to the road.

"Gosh! A *stamp*!" said Henry.

"An' she never even *read* all that hist'ry we put in,"

said William. "It was smashin' hist'ry an' she never even *read* it. All that trouble for nothin' an' we're jus' back where we started."

"Still—it was a good trick if it'd come off," said Henry wistfully.

"All that hist'ry wasted!" said William bitterly. "It's enough to put you off hist'ry for the rest of your life."

"An' we'll get into an awful row when she asks Miss Thompson about it an' finds out what happened," said Ginger.

"Oh, well," said William, "Miss Thompson's gone away for a fortnight so we needn't worry about that yet."

"One bridge at a time," said Henry.

A woman was coming down the road towards them. She was a pleasant-looking woman, with a kindly intelligent face. She stopped when she reached the group of boys and fixed her gaze on William.

"I've seen your photograph," she said. "It's William."

William eyed her with disfavour.

"An' I've seen yours," he said morosely. "It's Aunt Felicia."

"Yes, dear. I've just been to see your mother. I wanted to make a suggestion to her. I believe there's a rather thrilling Western on at the Hadley Cinema. I've forgotten its name——"

"*The Masked Ranger*," chorused the Outlaws.

"Yes, that's it. . . . Well, William, it occurred to me that we might go into Hadley after lunch and see the film. Would you like to?"

"Y-yes, please," said William.

"I believe it's a perfect horror, but I rather like horrors, don't you?"

"Y-yes," said William. "Yes, I do."

26

"Well, come to lunch with me as arranged and we'll go down to see the film afterwards. That all right? And now I must hurry to catch my bus."

She went on down the road. The world was spinning round William again.

"Gosh!" he said helplessly.

"You're goin' to *The Masked Ranger*, William," said Ginger, his voice breaking into a squeak of excitement.

"Yes," said William. Exhilaration leapt in him. "I'm goin' to *The Masked Ranger*." He attempted a handspring in the road and overbalanced. "I'm goin' to *The Masked Ranger*," he shouted exultantly as he picked himself up.

They separated for lunch. William walked homewards, still a little dazed. He realised suddenly that he had reached a stretch of road that always formed the background for some private drama. It had an overgrown dry ditch, a low tree overhanging the road and a hedge so bare at the roots that he could creep in and out of the holes. Generally he was a detective on the track of a criminal, or a criminal on the track of a detective, according to his mood. Today he was the Masked Ranger. Crouching in the ditch, he watched the Indians go past in single file. Hidden in the leafage of the tree, he took deadly aim at the black-hearted Indian chief. Pursued by the chief's infuriated tribesmen he dodged in and out of the holes, throwing them into wild confusion, and turning every now and then to take deadly aim at the nearest of his pursuers. It was while he was emerging from the last hole that he ran into Victor Jameson.

"Oh, hello," said Victor. "I forgot to tell you one part of *The Masked Ranger*. It was where he . . ."

"You needn't bother," said William. "I'll be seein' it on Saturday."

Victor stared at him, wide-eyed.

"I thought you weren't going," he said.

"Oh, I've fixed it," said William. "I'll be there with the others on Saturday."

Victor's eyes grew wider.

"How did you fix it?" he said.

William considered the question, at a loss for a moment how to answer it. Then he shrugged his shoulders and gave his short untuneful laugh.

"Oh, I've got *ways*," he said nonchalantly and continued his erratic progress down the road.

CHAPTER II

WILLIAM'S SUMMER HOLIDAY

"IT's quite nice, isn't it?" said William's mother, throwing open the door and entering the small bright sitting-room.

"Very nice," said Ginger's mother, following her into the room. "Not a view of the sea, of course, but it's only a short distance away."

They returned to the hall, where a pile of suitcases stood at the foot of the staircase.

"We'd better get unpacked," said Mrs. Brown. She went to the front door and called, "Come along, boys, and give a hand with the luggage."

William and Ginger came slowly up from the gate.

"It's nice, boys, isn't it?" said Mrs. Brown cheerfully.

"It's a house in a place," said William gloomily. "I jus' don't know why people want to go jus' from one house in one place to another in another."

"It's the summer holidays, dear," explained Mrs. Brown. "People *do*. . . . Now take the suitcases up to the bedrooms and be careful not to knock them against the wall. Then we'll unpack."

"I bet there won't be anythin' to do here," said William, grasping the handle of a suitcase.

"Packin' things jus' to unpack 'em," said Ginger with a careful imitation of William's gloom.

The Browns and the Merrydews had taken a furnished house at the seaside for a fortnight of the summer holiday. Mrs. Brown and Mrs. Merrydew, with William and Ginger, had come down that afternoon. and their husbands were to join them in the evening after their day's work.

"We'll do the unpacking now," said Mrs. Brown as William and Ginger came downstairs. "You two boys can go out and explore. Don't look so dismal, dear. I'm sure you'll find plenty to do for the fortnight we're here."

"A little change is good for all of us," said Mrs. Merrydew brightly.

William gave a short, sarcastic laugh, and Ginger his not very successful imitation of it.

"Now run along!" said Mrs. Brown.

The two set off slowly down the road. They had not wanted to come away from home. They had not wanted to leave the fields and woods of their beloved countryside. Their departure had meant abandoning several interesting activities in a maddeningly unfinished condition. There was the camp they were making in Coombe wood. There were the steps they were hacking out on the side of the old quarry in preparation for a mountaineering contest. There was the combined dam and fountain they were making in the stream that ran alongside the old barn. (Theoretically this was completed. Only a few prac-

29

tical difficulties remained to be overcome.) There was the new trick they were teaching Jumble. . . . The trick consisted of jumping through an old bicycle tyre, and Jumble was just beginning to have a dim idea of what was expected of him. Even Jumble had had to be left at home, because the owner of the furnished house had banned "pets". He had been left with Douglas, who was prepared to give his whole time to the care and entertainment of him, but his absence went to swell the sum of William's grievances. Moreover, the perennial feud with Hubert Lane was taking a new and interesting turn. Hubert had sent a challenge to William and his gang to meet him and his gang in the lane behind his house next Tuesday evening. It was obvious that some sinister plot was afoot, and William was rallying his gang to accept the challenge, prepared for any event.

The two walked on down the road, deaf and blind to their surroundings, their minds busied with their private problems.

"I bet someone finds that camp an' messes it all up," said William.

"An' we'll have to start makin' that fountain all over again," said Ginger.

"An' I bet Jumble'll have forgotten that trick. He won't do it for anyone but me, an' it took me *hours* teachin' him. An' I bet Douglas won't look after him prop'ly."

"He will," said Ginger earnestly. "He said he wouldn't let him out of his *sight*."

"Yes, an' that's goin'-to be jolly irritatin' for poor ole Jumble, isn't it, bein' stared at by Douglas all the time. . . . An' I bet Hubert Lane'll think we've gone away 'cause we're scared of him."

"No, he won't," said Ginger, "He——"

They stopped. They had come to a road junction. A small, battered signpost pointed "To the Beach."

"Come on," said William with a shrug. "Might as well go to it now we're here."

They walked down a narrow path to the top of a cliff.

Below them stretched a calm unruffled expanse of water.

"The sea," said Ginger.

"Well, I can see it, can't I?" said William. "I've got eyes, haven't I?"

He was looking at the sea with an expression of bored indifference. The sea, to William, meant storms, shipwrecks, pirates, smugglers, desert islands, torpedoes, desperate fights against desperate odds. He felt only contempt for this stretch of dimpled inanity.

"We could swim in it," suggested Ginger tentatively.

"We couldn't now," said William, "'cause our swimmin' things aren't unpacked." He shrugged. "Might as well go down to it, I s'pose."

They clambered down the cliff to the beach and walked along the sand.

"We could have finished that camp by now," said William morosely, "an' I bet it won't rain while we're here an' the ditch'll dry up an' there won't be enough water left to finish the fountain."

They stopped. The stretch of sand had come to an end and the sea ran inland between two tall cliff heads, forming a sort of river. On the other side, beach and cliff continued. The water, entering the narrow inlet, surged and eddied into waves.

Something of William's boredom dropped from him.

"That's a bit more like a sea," he said with grudging approval.

He looked at the further stretch of sand across the

31

strip of water. Fragments of flotsam and jetsam lay there, together with the litter of a recent picnic party: empty cartons, newspapers, and an old sack.

"We might be on a desert island," he said. "There's water nearly all round us. Gosh!" His excitement was rising. "Let's *pretend* we're on a desert island. What was that book someone read to us once about someone on a desert island that kept gettin' things off a wreck?"

Ginger considered for a moment, wrinkling his brows in thought.

"Robinson Crusoe," he said at last.

"Yes, that was it. Robinson Crusoe. He got saws an' hatchets an' muskets an' bullets an' provisions an' things off the wreck. . . . *Tell* you what! We'll pretend we're him on a desert island an' that the wreck's over there across the water. I can see lots of things we could pretend were hatchets an' things."

"We'll get a bit wet," said Ginger.

"Well, he didn't mind gettin' wet, so I don't see why we should. We'll take off our sandals then no one can say we didn't do our best."

They kicked off their sandals and set our across the strip of water. Ginger lost his foothold and grabbed hold of William, and the two were submerged for a moment in the swirling tide.

"That's all right," said William, regaining his foothold. "We've got wet now so we needn't bother about gettin' a bit wetter. Come on!"

They scrambled out on to the farthest shore and began to investigate the bits and pieces that lay scattered around.

"Look at this," said William, taking up a long jagged piece of wood. "It'll do for a saw"

Ginger had discovered a couple of liquorice all-sorts at the bottom of a paper bag.

"An' here's some provisions," he said, handing one to William and putting the other into his own mouth.

"An' here's a musket," said William, taking up a long narrow piece of driftwood.

"An' here's some shot," said Ginger, scooping up a handful of small stones.

"An' part of a sail," said William, taking up the old sack. "It'll do to make a tent. Now let's get back to the island. Come on."

They splashed their way back again over the stretch of water.

"Pity we couldn't find a dog or a parrot," said William.

"Or a Man Friday," said Ginger.

"Look!" said William excitedly.

He was pointing to tracks of bare feet that stretched along the beach.

"That wasn't there before," he said, "an' it's diff'rent from our feet."

"Man Friday," said Ginger in an awestruck whisper.

"Gosh, yes," said William, "an—*look!*—there he is!"

A boy was emerging from behind one of the rocks that lay at the foot of the cliff. He was about William's age, slender and wiry-looking, with coffee-coloured skin and bright dark eyes.

"Man Friday!" gasped Ginger again.

"He can't be Man Friday," said William, " 'cause he's not a man an' it's not Friday. It's Wednesday."

"Boy Wednesday, then," said Ginger.

The boy had joined them and was looking at them inquiringly.

"You're Boy Wednesday," said William.

The boy gave them a friendly smile and nodded his head in agreement.

"Me Boy Wednesday," he said.

33

He seemed pleased and flattered by the name.

"Well, come on with us," said William. "We'll go over to the wreck again an' try 'n' find somethin' else."

The boy seemed to grasp the situation. He splashed through the water with them, laughing happily when he tripped over a piece of rock and fell headlong.

"Me Boy Wednesday," he said proudly, as he picked himself up.

On the farther shore he watched William and Ginger intently for some moments then, with a quick flashing smile, set about imitating them, dragging up an armful of seaweed.

"Cabbage," he said gleefully. "From the wreck."

"He's jolly good," said Ginger. "We were lucky to find him . . . Hope he's not a cannibal, though. The one in the book was."

"Well, he'll have a job eating the two of us. even if he is," said William with a chuckle.

They watched him as he burrowed beneath the sodden newspaper and brought out an empty milk bottle.

"Telescope from the wreck," he said, putting it to his eye.

"Yes, he's cert'nly all right," said William in a tone of finality. "Come on. Let's get some more stuff."

William found a few more pieces of driftwood and Ginger half a ragged towel.

"Wood to make a fence to keep off wild animals," said William.

"An' a flag for a signal to passing ships," said Ginger.

"From the wreck," said Wednesday.

Laden with their spoils, they returned to the desert island.

"The man in that book . . ." said William. "What was he called again?"

34

"You're Boy Wednesday," said William.

"Robinson Crusoe."

"Yes, him. Well, he chose a sort of cave in the rocks an' made a fence of wood an' then put big stones all round it. Look! Here's a sort of cave. It goes right back into the cliff. Let's stick up the bits of wood for a fence an' then find some stones."

Ginger looked round the deserted beach.

"Boy Wednesday's gone," he said.

"Oh, well . . ." said William, "we'll get on all right without him. Let's start puttin' up the fence."

They worked in silence for some time, then an exultant shout rang out and they turned to see Boy Wednesday nimbly descending the cliff with two paper bags in his mouth.

He approached them and laid the paper bags at their feet.

"From the wreck," he said proudly.

William opened the bags. One contained biscuits and the other tomatoes.

"Where did you get them from?" said William.

But Wednesday was already scaling the cliff again and almost out of sight.

"He's pinched them from somewhere," said Ginger with a note of apprehension in his voice.

William shrugged.

"Well, we might as well eat 'em," he said. "No good wastin' them. We'll leave him his share 'case he comes back."

He divided the biscuits and tomatoes into three portions.

"He might be a spy, of course," said William, "sent out by some native tribe. They could hide up anywhere on a desert island, an' they might attack us any minute." He put a couple of chocolate biscuits into his mouth and continued indistinctly. "We'll jus' have to keep a look-out an' listen for their war cry."

They finished the tomatoes and biscuits and went on with the work of setting up the "fence".

Suddenly another exultant cry rang out and they saw Wednesday nimbly descending the cliff again. A battered rush basket hung over his shoulders. He clambered over the rocks to them and laid the basket at their feet.

"From the wreck," he said with a radiant smile.

"He's all right," said William. "He's not a spy."

"Yes, but he's pinchin' things," said Ginger. "Dunno where he's pinchin' them from but he's pinchin' 'em all right."

William handed the tomatoes and biscuits to Wednesday.

"Eat 'em," he said.

Wednesday bit zestfully into a tomato.

"He's jolly intelligent," said William, surveying his new acquisition with an air of proprietorship. "An' he isn't a spy *or* a cannibal. Come on—let's see what's in the basket."

He opened the basket and drew out the contents—a large, dilapidated tweed cap, an equally dilapidated muffler, an unsavoury-looking clay pipe and three highly polished apples.

"From the wreck," said Wednesday again, through a mouthful of tomato.

He appeared to think that the words gave a full and complete account of the situation.

Then he reached out a hand, took the cap and put it on his head, drawing it so far down that he had to tilt up his head to grin at them.

"Me Boy Wednesday," he said delightedly.

Ginger swathed the dilapidated muffler round his neck

and William plunged the unsavoury-looking clay pipe into his mouth. They chuckled in enjoyment of the joke for some moments then William stood up and surveyed the landscape.

"I'm gettin' a bit tired of this ole wreck business," he said, removing his pipe with a flourish. "Let's have a go at explorin' the interior of the island Let's climb the cliff. Come on."

"Me climb," said Wednesday eagerly, starting to his feet and slinging the basket over his shoulder again.

There was no doubt that Wednesday was a more skilled climber than either William or Ginger. They followed him, using the footholds he used, pulling themselves up by the same ledges.

On the top of the cliff a stretch of grass seemed to lead to a small village.

"Come on," said William. "Let's start explorin'."

They took the path across the grassy cliff-top and came to a stile. On the other side of the stile was a country road leading to a little group of shops.

Ginger began to unwind his scarf.

"Better keep it on," said William. "It'll do as a sort of disguise."

William puffed violently at his clay pipe. and Wednesday drew his cap still farther over his eyes. Then Wednesday unslung the basket from his shoulder.

"To eat," he said. "From the wreck."

"Gosh, yes," said William. "The apples. I forgot those. Better eat 'em to stop 'em goin' bad."

They walked on towards the shops, each munching an apple.

Outside the grocer's a woman was holding forth to a little group of people, pointing dramatically to a shopping basket on wheels.

"I met Mrs. Smith and we just had a little chat, standing here like this. I only turned my back on it for a couple of minutes while I chatted to her and—would you believe it!—when I turned round my tomatoes and biscuits had gone. Just gone! They'd been *taken* by someone in just those few minutes while my back was turned. Would you *believe* it!"

"It's this wave of crime," said another woman sombrely. "It's sweeping the whole country."

The three boys sloped past with averted heads.

"I *knew* he'd pinched them," said Ginger. "He'll get us into trouble before he's finished."

They walked on, past the shops, down a road that was skirted by a high brick wall, and stopped at an imposing-looking pair of gates, which bore a notice "Highlands School. Headmaster: Arnold J. Mercer, M.A.".

"Gosh, a *school*!" said William in a tone of disgust. "Let's get away from it quick."

But the building seemed to hold a morbid fascination for Ginger.

"Let's jus' have a look at it," he said. "Let's jus' see what it's like. It's the holidays. No one'll be about."

Slowly, fearfully, they entered the gate and began to walk up the drive, still munching their apples, craning their necks round the bend that half hid, half revealed the large square house.

"Gosh, doesn't it look awful!" said Ginger.

"It looks jus' like a school," said William. "You can tell 'em anywhere."

"Me no like school," said Wednesday, wrinkling his nose under the all-enveloping cap.

Suddenly a bellow of rage sounded behind them, and they turned to see a small, crab-like figure coming after them. His face was congested with fury, and he waved his arms in windmill motions as he ran. The bellows of rage continued to fill the air, and, despite his small, crab-like figure, he covered the ground with unexpected rapidity.

The three boys dodged round to the back of the house. A high wall surrounded the back garden, broken by a green painted gate. William hurled himself at the green painted gate. It was locked. They looked desperately around. The crab-like figure and bellows of rage were hot on their tracks. Suddenly the crab-like figure tripped over a rake that lay across the path and for a second or two lost sight of the boys.

"Quick!" gasped William. "Get behind that heap."

The three plunged behind a compost heap that stood close to the wall.

The crab-like figure had scrambled to its feet and was now peering into a small tool-shed, uttering low ferocious growls.

"He'll be here in a minute," said William. "Let's get right into it."

He crawled into the compost heap. The others did the same, covering themselves up as best they could with the dark moist mixture.

The crab-like figure passed the heap, throwing a cursory glance at the passage between it and the wall, then went on, still growling ferociously.

William emerged and looked cautiously around.

"He's not anywhere about," he reported. "We'd better come out an' get away as quick as we can."

Slowly the other two appeared. It was a rich fruity compost, and it clung to their persons in clumps and smears and patches. They shook themselves without much result. Wednesday drew his ill-fitting, evil-smelling cap down over his face and chuckled. Ginger tightened his

*Slowly, fearfully, they entered the gate and
began to walk up the drive.*

scarf about his neck. William's pipe and the remainder of
the apples were lost in the decaying mass.

"I can't see him anywhere," said William. His eyes
rested hopefully on a strip of shrubs and young trees
that ran along the side of the lawn. "We could creep
along to the front through that an' dash out of the gate.
Come on! Creep on your stomachs like Indians."

They crept on their stomachs from shrub to shrub,
towards the house. The approach to the house brought
them close to a large bay window that overlooked the
lawn. William, whose interest in his fellow creatures was

41

unquenchable, stopped for a moment behind a holly bush to examine as much as he could see of the interior of the room, despite the hazards that surrounded him.

It was a large book-lined room, with a writing-desk at the window and, in the middle, a heavy oak table at which three men were sitting. One was thick-set and keen-eyed, the second tall, young, dark-skinned and elegantly dressed, the third middle-aged, with untidy grey hair and a square, kindly, harassed-looking face. The keen-eyed man was settling himself in a chair as if he had just arrived.

"They look as if they were talkin' about somethin' interestin'," said William. "Pity we can't hear them."

William was right. They were talking about something interesting.

"Now, Mr. Mercer," the keen-eyed man was saying as he drew a notebook from his pocket. "Let's get the facts down. You expected the boy today?"

"Yes, Inspector," said the harassed-looking man. "I expected him this morning. My school broke up for the summer holidays last week, you know." The Inspector nodded. "But, as you probably also know, I always take in a number of boys for the summer holidays. Boys whose parents are abroad or cannot make any other arrangements for them. We have games, activities of various sorts, excursions. . . . A sort of holiday home."

Again the Inspector nodded.

"Well, this boy," went on Mr. Mercer, "was to have arrived this morning to join the school for the summer holidays. Perhaps Mr. Nassir here"—he waved a hand towards the dark skinned, elegantly dressed man—"had better explain the situation."

The dark skinned man had evidently no objection to

42

doing this. He spread out his hands in an eloquent gesture.

"I am secretary to the ambassador of our country to your country, and my employer has only lately been appointed to the position and has not yet been able to organise his domestic affairs. He wished to place his son in Mr. Mercer's care for the summer holidays while he found a suitable house and school in London. He is so engrossed with political matters that he has not yet had time to organise his own private matters and——"

Suddenly the door burst open and a small crab-like figure appeared, its face distorted by rage.

"What is it, Craig?" said Mr. Mercer patiently.

"Them boys, sir! Them varmints!" spluttered Craig. "Pinched me bag with me cap an' me muffler an' me pipe in it. *An'* me apples that I was puttin' in for the Flower Show. *Eatin'* me prize apples, they were, the little divils, an'——"

"Now listen, Craig," said Mercer. "You'll never win a prize with those Worcesters of yours. Major Forrester's are twice the size——"

"I'd got me basket ready for me work," said Craig, his voice breaking on a shrill note of fury, "with me cap an' me muffler an' me pipe an'——"

"Craig," said Mr. Mercer, "can't you see I'm busy now?"

"I can't work without me cap an' me pipe an' me muffler. I get the rheumatics crule without me cap an' me muffler."

"We'll go into this later, Craig."

"I'd got to the gate all set to come out to work with 'em all in me basket——"

"Craig, I can't possibly go into all this now."

"Then I bethought meself that I hadn't let the cat out, so I puts down me basket an' goes back to let the cat out an' when I comes back to the gate it'd gone—me basket with me cap, me muffler, me pipe, me prize apples an'——"

"Please go away now, Craig."

"I knowed some of them young divils had done it an' I seed 'em, bold as brass, wearin' me cap an' me muffler——"

"*Craig!*"

"Smokin' me pipe, eatin' me apples——"

Mr. Mercer rose to his feet, advanced upon his visitor, pushed him firmly out of the room and closed the door.

"I must apologise for the interruption, gentlemen," he said, returning to his seat. "Craig is the gardener here and quite invaluable, but he's an odd character—a little subnormal, I suppose—and he has a running feud with the village boys. They tease and torment him just to get him into a rage. I suppose they've been taking his precious cap and muffler. He wears them invariably at work, whatever the weather. . . . I'll deal with it later, of course. Meantime let's get back to the matter in hand."

"Certainly," said the Inspector with a touch of impatience. "Will you continue, Mr. Nassir?"

"Everything was arranged," said Mr. Nassir, "and I was to bring the boy down to Highlands today. Unfortunately, most unfortunately, we found ourselves devoid of petrol only a few miles from here and I set out to walk to a garage we had passed recently and, when I returned with the petrol"—he threw out his arms in a despairing gesture—"the boy had gone."

"I take it you made a thorough search of the place," said the Inspector.

"Yes, indeed. Indeed, yes. A most thorough search.

But I wanted to report the affair at once so I came swiftly here to Mr. Mercer for his advice."

"Have you got into touch with the boy's father?" said the Inspector.

Mr. Nassir made a frantic gesture of denial.

"No, indeed. Indeed, no. His position is a delicate one needing all his time and energy. To inform him of Abdullah's vanishing would send him, as you say in this country, beyond the bend. He is devoted to the boy. He would break off all those delicate negotiations on which the fate and future of our country depend to come here and search for the boy. He would dismiss me from my employment. He would suffer physical and mental breakdown. He would not eat nor sleep. He would care for nothing till the boy was found."

"Yes, yes," said the Inspector soothingly. "Now just a few more questions. Was the boy dressed in any distinctive way?"

"Indeed, no," sighed Mr. Nassir. "He refused to wear the appropriate suit of grey flannel that we purchased for him. He insisted on wearing the shorts and the shirt, having seen other boys in this country thus attired. We argued, but in vain. He is a determined child. Charming— but determined. I was unwilling for some time to agree to consult the police."

"Why were you unwilling?" said the Inspector.

"More is involved than you can know," said Mr. Nassir, sinking his voice to a low mysterious whisper. "There are dark forces at work, wheels within secret wheels, underground plots, villainous conspiracies . . ."

"What Mr. Nassir means," put in the Headmaster, "is that he's afraid the boy's been kidnapped."

"Kidnapped?" said the Inspector sharply.

"Well, you know what it is in these newly independent countries," said the Headmaster. "A frantic struggle for power. Presidents changed overnight. Half a dozen different parties trying to get into the saddle. . . . Mr. Nassir says that the boy's father has enemies who may have followed him to England. He supported the present president against the last president and he's afraid that the kidnapping may be an act of revenge by the followers of the last president."

"I see . . ." said the Inspector. "Now where exactly did you leave the child, Mr. Nassir?"

"Not very far from here," said Mr. Nassir. "We had in fact almost completed our journey when unfortunately —most unfortunately—I realised that my petrol gauge was not acting correctly and that I was devoid of petrol. The garage was only a short distance down the road and I was away only a few moments."

"Did any other car pass down the road?" said the Inspector.

"That I cannot be sure of. I went into the office of the garage to explain the situation. A car, of course, might have passed while I was thus engaged."

"Well, we oughtn't to waste any more time," said the Inspector. "I must alert the whole district and, of course, the boy's father must be informed at once."

"No, no," wailed Mr. Nassir, clasping his hands beseechingly. "I beg and implore you, not yet. He is engaged in delicate negotiations. The fate of our country trembles in the balance. And—and I should lose my job, which I value deeply." He flung his arms out in another eloquent gesture. "Oh, I would give all I possess in the world to see the child again."

"I can assure you that no effort will be spared to find him," said the Inspector, "but——"

The door burst open and Craig appeared again, pushing in front of him a small unsightly object. In his eagerness to secure justice, he had not stopped to remove the cap, and his grasp on the collar had sent it forward, completely obscuring the boy's features. The rest of his person was still thickly plastered with compost.

"What on earth is the meaning of this?" stormed the Headmaster.

"I got one of 'em," panted Craig. "The worst of the lot, the little varmint! I told 'im I'd bring 'im to you. I told 'im you'd larn 'im. I told 'im——"

The Headmaster's exasperation broke its bounds.

"How *dare* you come in here again like this!" he said. "Take the wretched boy away. Take him to the gate and send him right off. As for you"—he glared down at the all enveloping cap—"don't you ever *dare* come here again! Off with you!"

With a swift eel-like movement the boy freed himself from Craig's grasp and slipped out through the doorway.

"But listen, sir——" began Craig.

"Go away!" bellowed the Headmaster.

Craig went away.

"I apologise once more for the interruption," said the Headmaster. "Now what's the next step?"

"Well, I'll give you half an hour before I set the wheels in motion," said the Inspector. "If he's not found in half an hour, I'm afraid we must inform his father and make the matter public."

"It will kill him," wailed Mr. Nassir.

"Don't worry, sir," said the Inspector reassuringly. "After all, the boy can't be far away."

The boy was not far away. He was in fact only a few yards from the window of the room where he was being discussed. He had already joined William and Ginger behind the holly bush.

"I escaped him," he panted as he joined them. "I escaped him, but he still seeks us. He——"

"Sh!" said Ginger. "Here he comes!"

Craig was approaching with his crab-like gait, peering into the shrubs.

"I know you're somewhere about, you little divils, you!" he growled. "Wait till I gets holt o' you! Jus' you wait till I gets holt o' you."

He went down towards the end of the garden, still muttering and peering . . .

"Look!" whispered William. "The garage door's open an' there's a car in it. We can get right up to it behind the bushes. Let's creep into it an' hide. I bet no one'll be goin' out in the car. They're all too busy talkin' in that room. We'll get in the back an' stay there till he's tired of lookin' for us, then we'll slip out of the gate. He'll never think of lookin' in the car. Come on!"

Silently, in single file, sheltering behind each bush as they came to it, they made their way into the garage. A small four-seater stood there.

"Let's get in the back," said William, "an' cover ourselves up with the rug."

They got on to the floor of the back of the car and covered themselves with the thick tartan rug. There was not much room and they found themselves uncomfortably crowded.

"Take your foot off my neck," said Ginger. "I can't breathe."

"Shut up!" said William.

Footsteps were approaching. William peeped cautiously out from a corner of the rug. Three men had entered the garage.

"Gosh!" he breathed in dismay, diving beneath the rug again.

"I suggest that you drive to the point in the road where you missed the child," said the Inspector. "He may, of course, have found his way back there or the people

He pulled off the rug and dragged out the three boys.

at the garage may have some news of him. Meantime, I'll ring up the station—if I may use your telephone, Mr. Mercer—and give a few discreet instructions, then I'll follow you in my car. We oughtn't to waste any more time."

The Headmaster and Mr. Nassir got into the car and

drove quickly through the village to the road that ran along the top of the cliff. The three boys in the back of the car crouched there, silent and immobile. They had surrendered themselves to fate.

"It was just here," said Mr. Nassir suddenly. The car came to a stop. "It was here that I got out to walk to the garage. You do not see the garage from here, but——"

"What on *earth*——!" said the Headmaster.

He had suddenly noticed strange writhing movements beneath the rug, as Ginger forcibly removed William's foot from his neck. He pulled off the rug and dragged out the three boys. He dragged out Abdullah last. The cap had become detached from his head, and the delicate if grimy features were plainly recognisable.

"Abdullah!" cried Mr. Nassir hysterically.

With a sudden unexpected movement Abdullah butted Mr. Mercer in the stomach with his head and set off at a run towards the cliff edge. The Headmaster collapsed in a sitting position on the grass verge. Mr. Nassir sprinted lightly after the small fleeing figure, caught it by the collar and brought it back.

"Now Abdullah——"

"Me Boy Wednesday," put in Abdullah hotly.

"You must come at once back to the school. Do you understand?"

Abdullah shrugged. He had had a good run for his money, but he realised that circumstances had beaten him.

"But, first of all, Abdullah——"

"Me Boy Wednesday," said Abdullah. His eyes flashed fiercely. "Me *Boy Wednesday*."

"Well-er-Wednesday, you must apologise to this gentle-
50

man"—the Headmaster had scrambled to his feet—"for your ungentlemanly behaviour."

Abdullah inclined his head in Mr. Mercer's direction.

"I pardon you," he said, adding with his sudden charming smile, "freely".

William and Ginger entered the sitting-room. They had brushed each other down in a rough and ready fashion, removing the more detachable portions of the compost heap, but they presented, none the less, a deplorable spectacle.

"My goodness!" said Mrs. Merridew. "What *have* you been doing! Go and wash and change at once."

"You certainly are in a mess," said Mrs. Brown more mildly. "You've evidently explored the countryside pretty thoroughly, and I hope you've found that there'll be something for you to do during the two weeks we're here."

William's mind went back over the afternoon. Reluctantly and with obvious misgiving, the Headmaster had yielded to Abdullah's insistence that William and Ginger should be allowed to come to Highlands to play with him during the rest of their stay. On their way home they had met the coach bringing the other boys who were coming to spend their holiday (or part of their holiday) at Highlands. Two of them were fighting. Another was playing a mouth organ. Another was plastering his neighbour's hair with the inside of a banana skin. A boy who was the living image of Hubert Lane threw a challenging grimace at William as they passed. It was a coachful of glorious possibilities.

"Oh, yes," said William as he turned towards the door. "Yes, I think we're goin' to find quite a lot to do for the two weeks we're here."

51

CHAPTER III

WILLIAM AND THE DONKEY

"HE came to dinner with my fam'ly yesterday," said Henry, "and he's a man that *knows*."

"Knows what?" said William.

"Knows what he's talkin' about. He only jus' didn't get into Parliament an' he's on a committee for savin' the countryside."

"That's pretty good," said Douglas, impressed.

"But what did he *say*?" said William.

"I'm tryin' to tell you," said Henry. "It's somethin' jolly important an' it may mean trag'dy for all of us."

"Well, go on! *Tell* us," said Ginger.

"Well, he said he used to live in a house in the middle of fields an' woods an' he went away on a holiday an' when he came back he found the fields all dug up an' the woods all cut down an' houses all over the place an' he said it might happen to *anyone*."

The four were sitting in the old barn. William threw a glance at the open doorway that framed a sunlit expanse of fields and hedges, with stretches of woodland in the distance.

"Well, no one's buildin' round here," he said, "so *we're* all right, anyway."

"So far," said Henry. "Only so far. He said, this man, that *anyone* might wake up one mornin' an' find houses goin' up all over the place an', once they've started, it's too late to stop 'em 'cause of these plans."

"What plans?" said William.

"They make plans for buildin' houses." said Henry. "Sort of drawings of them, you know, an' they take them to a meeting of the mayor an' corporation an' they pass them an', once these plans have been passed, no one can stop 'em building them."

"Can't people go to this meetin' an' stop the mayor an' corporation passin' them?" said William.

"Yes, they could, but ordin'ry people don't go to meetings 'cause they've not got time, so the nex' thing they know is they wake up one mornin' an' find houses all round 'em and all the fields an' woods gone an'—an' it might happen to *anyone*. It might happen to *us*. *We* might wake up one mornin' an' find houses all over our fields."

"P'raps they'd jus' leave us the barn," said Douglas pathetically.

"No, they wouldn't," said Henry. "This man said there was a picturesque barn in one of the fields next his house, an' they jus' pulled it down."

The faces of the Outlaws froze with horror.

They had taken the old barn—a derelict, tumble-down structure in a corner of the field—for granted. It had been their refuge, their meeting place, the background of all their adventures ever since they could remember. They had planned their most daring *coups* in it, hidden from their enemies in it, used it as a ship, aeroplane, desert island; headquarters of pirates, robbers, spies and even Scotland Yard itself. It partook of the nature of home for them more than those neat dwellings where they ate and slept and conformed—in a greater or lesser degree— to the rule of Authority. They had taken all this for granted. They hadn't thought about it—till today. And today—faced by the monstrous possibility of its loss— they were dumbfounded and appalled.

"An' there's *nothin*' we can do," wailed Douglas.

But already William's features were gathering themselves into the tight knot of resolution that never failed to reassure them and, as they watched him, something of their gloom lightened.

"Well, it can't happen as quick as all that," he said. "I mean, they can't build fieldfuls of houses all in one night. They'd have to do a bit of measurin' up first an' we'll see 'em doin' it."

"An' what'll we do *then*?" said Ginger. "We can't fight a whole mayor an' corporation."

"Oh, we'll find a way all right," said William, "I'm jolly well not scared of any ole mayor an' corporation. They're only *people* same as us."

"But what'll we *do*?" persisted Ginger.

"The first thing to do is to keep a look-out," said William. "Now listen! We'll have one of us on guard all the time so's they can't start anythin' without us knowin', an' as soon as we see anyone measurin it up—well, we'll lay our plans."

"We haven't a hope," said Douglas dismally.

"We've got right on our side," said Henry.

For the next week the Outlaws patrolled the fields round the old barn daily. They had decided reluctantly not to carry arms or wear disguises. These things appealed to their sense of the dramatic, but might have drawn attention to their movements and might even have attracted the eye of some land-hungry builder to the desirable site afforded by the fields.

At first they examined every inch of field and ditch for traces of possible surveyors, scrutinising every corner of the old barn with the help of Henry's magnifying glass,

54

tracking down the most innocent inhabitants who used the short cut across the fields to reach their homes. But after a week or so these activities began to pall. Other interests claimed their time and energy. Their first fine zest was flagging, and the lack of any signs of house-building brought an element of flatness into the situation.

"We can't go on watchin' grass for the rest of our lives," said William irritably. "It'd send us dotty never doin' anythin' for the rest of our lives but watchin' grass an' lookin' out for people that don't come. We can't waste our whole *lives* on it. I vote we stop for a bit an' jus' go on same as we used to. We can go to the old barn when we want to an' not when we don't. . . . We never finished that control tower we were makin' in Ginger's tree."

The others agreed with something of relief.

"There's a time and a place for everything," said Henry with his wonted air of philosophic wisdom.

"I jus' about know every insect in those fields by now," said Douglas. "I'm gettin' sick of their faces an' I bet they're gettin' sick of mine."

"Well, you wouldn't need to be an insect to do *that*," said William with heavy sarcasm, starting a hilarious scuffle in which all four joined.

So it was quite by accident that William, walking along the road a few days later, carrying an ancient discarded fireguard to assist in the construction of the control tower, noticed the two men in the field beside the old barn. One was a tall man with grey hair and bushy eyebrows, and the other was small and squat with a black beard. The grey-haired man was holding the end of a long measuring tape and the bearded man was stooping down at the other end. Then they rolled the measure into its case and stood together, while the grey-haired man made notes in an official-looking notebook, raising his eyes every now and

55

then to throw glances of frowning calculation round the field.

William's heart seemed to stop beating. He stood there, staring over the hedge, his mouth open, his face blank with dismay. Then he dropped his fireguard into the ditch, crossed the stile and, hands in pockets, mouth pursed in an untuneful whistle, eyes fixed vacantly on the distance, made his way to where the two men stood, and hovered within earshot, absorbed apparently in pulling his socks from their usual position round his ankles to a more correct adjustment. They threw him careless glances and continued their conversation.

"We could get six in there," said the grey-haired man, pointing round the old barn.

"Easily," said the other man. He waved his hand in the direction of the hedge. "And we could make an entrance there and get another six in the farther field."

William had heard enough. Abandoning his pose of indifference, he ran down the field, scrambled over the stile and made off for Ginger's house. He found Ginger, Henry and Douglas in Ginger's garden. They stood in a little group at the foot of the chestnut tree, where they had assembled various oddments—an old tyre, a packing-case, a pair of steps, several planks and a disintegrating garden chair—for the construction of the control tower.

"Where's your fireguard?" said Ginger.

"Never mind the fireguard," said William breathlessly. "They've started."

"Started what?"

"Started buildin' houses, of course. They're puttin' six of them in our field an' six in the next."

They stared at him, aghast.

"Gosh!"

"So we've got to *stop* 'em," said William. "We've got

to stop 'em before they take the plans to the mayor an' corporation meetin'. They've only jus' started so we've got to stop 'em before they can go any further."

"How?" said Henry.

"Now listen," said William. His face was stern and resolute. They gathered closely round him. "This man

William's heart seemed to stop beating.

with grey hair was the architect. He mus' have been 'cause he was measurin' up the ground an' makin' notes, so he's the one we've got to stop. If he doesn't make the plans they can't build the houses. Stands to reason. So we've got to stop him makin' the plans."

"How?" said Henry again.

"Well, we've got to find out about him first," said

William. "We've got to find out who he is an' where he lives."

"Is he anyone we know?" said Douglas.

"What did you say he looked like?" said Ginger.

"He had grey hair an' big black eyebrows," said William.

"Gosh, I've *seen* a man like that," said Henry excitedly. "He lives in Marleigh in that house opposite the church."

"Come on, then," said William in a brisk business-like voice. "Let's go'n' have a look. There's no time to lose. He might be makin' those plans this very minute an' they might have 'em *built* by the end of the week."

They set off briskly down the road, pausing at the stile to look at the fields. The two men had gone. The fields were empty. The old barn seemed to doze peacefully in the sunshine. They threw sorrowful glances in its direction as they passed.

"Gosh!" said Ginger. "It's the sort of thing you jus' can't believe."

"We're not goin' to believe it," said William stoutly. "We're goin' to *stop* it."

They slackened their pace as they reached Marleigh church, and stood in the shadow of the lych gate, gazing at the house opposite.

It was a small ivy-coloured Georgian house, set back in a shady garden. It bore the name "Ivy Lodge" on the gate. A man was bending over one of the borders, busy with hoe and trowel.

"Is he the man?" whispered Henry to William.

"Yes, he is," said William.

"He looks pretty strong," said Douglas. "I don't think it'd be any good tryin' to kidnap him."

" 'Course it wouldn't " said William. "We've got to think out somethin' better than that."

"Somethin' subtle," said Henry, pronouncing the word as spelt.

"We don't even know he's the architect yet," said Ginger.

"He mus' be," said William.

"He'd have a brass plate on his gate if he was," said Douglas, "same as a dentist, an' I can't see one."

"It may be on his front door," said William. "We can't see that from here. Let's go closer an' have a look."

They crossed the road and stood in the gateway of Ivy Lodge. The man looked up at them then put down his hoe and came towards the gate.

"Can I do anything for you," he said.

"Well," said William politely, "we were jus' wonderin' if you were an architect."

"Yes, I'm an architect," said the man. "Anderson by name." His eyes twinkled. "Are you requiring anything in the house-building line?"

"No, we're jolly well *not*," said Ginger fiercely.

"Shut up," said William under his breath. He fixed the architect with what was meant to be an ingratiating smile. "We—we're jus' sort of int'rested in architecture, that's all. We—we thought we might learn a bit about it, 'case we want to be one when we grow up."

"An excellent idea," said the man. The church clock sent out four resonant notes. He looked at his watch. "Good Lord! I forgot my watch was slow. I have to catch a train. . . . Yes, it's an interesting profession, but there's not much scope for it these days. Everything's too much regimented and—well, I must hurry off. Good-bye."

He took up hoe and trowel and disappeared round the side of the house.

"Well, we've not done much good by *that*," said Douglas.

"We jolly well *have*," said William. "We've found out he's the man that's plannin' those houses an' now we've got to——"

"To lay our counterplot," supplied Henry.

"Yes, an' it was jolly cunnin' of me to tell him we were int'rested in architecture. We can talk to him about it now any time we like."

"An' how's *that* goin' to help?" said Douglas.

"I'll tell you . . ." said William, "but we won't stay here any longer now. We don't want him to get suspicious of us. Come on. Let's go back to the old barn an' have a meeting."

They walked slowly across the fields towards the old barn.

"He seemed quite a nice man," said Ginger.

"That was his cunnin'," said William.

"It's the ones that seem nice that are always blackest at heart," said Henry.

They reached the old barn and took their seats for the meeting—William and Henry on the two packing-cases, Ginger and Douglas on the ground.

"Now listen," said William. "That man's the one that's goin' to make the plans for those houses. We've found that out an' it gives us a jolly good start. Well, if he doesn't make the plans they can't build the houses 'cause there won't be any plans for this mayor an' corporation to pass."

"But if he *wants* to make plans——" began Henry.

"We've got to stop him *wantin'* to make plans," said William. "We can't stop him makin'. plans if he wants to, but we've got to stop him *wantin'* to."

"How?" said Henry.

"Scare him off," said William.

"Scare him off?"

"Yes," said William. "We've got to think out a way to scare him off. Let's think out some awful things that have happened to people in houses to scare him off."

"Murders an' hauntin's," said Ginger.

"Yes, we could try those," said William, "an' I re-

"We've got to stop him wantin' *to make plans,"*
said William.

member there was an old tomb somewhere abroad that anyone that had anythin' to do with it came to a ghastly end."

"Yes, I remember," said Henry. "It was an Egyptian tomb."

"An' I once read about a jewel that came off an idol,"

61

said Ginger, "an' sent everyone ravin' mad that tried to wear it. An' that's *true*, 'cause a boy told me about it that knew a man that knew a man it happened to. He was a boy I met on a holiday at the seaside an' "—he chuckled—"he tried to push me off the prom into the sea an' fell in himself."

"I dunno that we could use that on a house," said William doubtfully.

"We could try," said Ginger.

"An' there's black magic," said Henry.

"What's that?" said William.

"It's to do with devils," said Henry. "If people did black magic in the old days in those fields then anyone that built houses on 'em or tried to live in 'em—well, they'd be haunted by devils all their lives. There's black magic signs, too, that breathe out evil an' make your blood run cold an' bring the most ghastly bad luck, so that everythin' you do turns to wrack an' ruin."

"That's jolly good," said William. "We'll try 'em all. You tell him about the hauntin', Henry, an' Ginger about the tomb an' Douglas the jewel an' I'll do the black magic, an' I bet we get him so scared that he'll never make any more plans for the rest of his life."

"I bet he won't listen," said Douglas.

"Yes, he will," said William. "I'll be specially polite so he'll have to."

They met the next morning and made their way across the fields to Marleigh. They found the architect perched on a ladder in the road, trimming his hedge.

William approached and cleared his throat on a strange barking note that made the man turn round with a start.

"Hello," he said. "The budding architects! Well, well, well!"

Then he turned round and continued his hedge-cutting.

The Outlaws felt a little nonplussed.

William cleared his throat again in a higher and yet more arresting key.

"We jus' want to ask you a few questions about architecture," he said, baring his teeth in the ingratiating smile, "if it's not too much trouble. I mean, 'scuse us int'ruptin' you."

"Certainly," said the man, bending down to attack a particularly strong growth that protruded from the lower part of the hedge.

"Well," said William, "you know those fields with the old barn in 'em?"

"I think so," said the man.

William gave a harsh laugh.

"Well, I'm jolly sorry for anyone that tries to build houses in 'em," he said.

"Why?" said the man.

"Go on," whispered William, nudging Henry.

"There's been murders done there," said Henry. "Murders an'—an' deeds of darkness. It's dyed in blood, an' haunted by the most ghastly spectres. No one'd be able to sleep at night in a house built on 'em an' anyone who *built* houses on 'em—well, his doom'd be sealed soon as he started."

"Really?" said the man absently.

His whole attention was now given to an uneven patch of hedge just above his head.

William made an urgent grimace in Ginger's direction and pushed him towards the hedge.

"An'—an' there's a sort of hollow place in the field," said Ginger. "You can hear it's hollow when you knock on it an'—well, it sounds to me jus' like an old Egyptian tomb an' if any one starts diggin' there to make houses they'll be struck dead or driven stark starin' mad."

"Just stand back a bit, will you?" said the man. "I want to see if I've got this bit quite straight. . . . Pass me the scissors from the wheelbarrow, will you?"

William passed the scissors and gave Douglas a nudge.

"Go on!" he whispered urgently.

"I—I've got a sort of idea," stammered Douglas, "that there's jewels hidden there off an idol an'—an' Ginger met a man that had one of these jewels an' got pushed off the promenade into the sea."

"I did *not*," said Ginger fiercely. "You've got it all wrong."

"Shut up!" said William.

But it was obvious that the man was not listening to them. He was bending sideways, trimming the last uneven patch with frowning concentration.

"An' there's black magic," said William.

The man came down the ladder and looked at them, giving them, as it seemed, his full attention for the first time.

"What about it?" he said.

He took two slats of wood from the barrow and began to collect the scattered hedge-cuttings.

"It can do the most ghastly things to people," said William. "It can get them tortured by devils so's they die in ag'ny or it can turn them into devils so's they can't get back."

"Sounds most unpleasant," said the man, putting another pile of hedge-cuttings into the wheelbarrow.

"Well, s'pose," said William, sinking his voice to a deep sinister note, "s'pose you were makin' a plan of a house an' black magic signs kept comin' on it an' every time you made a fresh one, *still* black magic signs kept

"An' there's black magic," said William.

C

comin' on it so's you could hardly *see* it for black magic signs, would you go on buildin' the house in spite of it?"

The man stood for a few moments in silent consideration.

"No, I don't think I would," he said at last. "No I'm quite sure I wouldn't." He put his shears into the wheelbarrow and took up the handles "Well, I think I've done all I can do here for the present. Good day to you."

"Good day," said the Outlaws and watched him as he trundled the barrow round the side of the house.

William turned to the others.

"Well," he said, "*now* we know what to do. It's as plain as *plain*. We've got to get those plans he's made of those houses an' put black magic signs all over 'em an' then he'll be so scared he'll tear them all up an' if there aren't any plans they can't build the houses."

They looked at him, bewildered and only half convinced.

"We can't make black magic signs," said Henry.

"I bet I can," said William. "I can draw little devils in red ink that look jus' like real ones. I'm jolly good at red devils I did some in my hist'ry book an' old Frenchie was mad about it, but I bet he was scared all the same. Now all we've got to do is to get hold of those plans an' I'll draw red devils all over them an' he'll be so scared he'll stop 'em buildin' the houses."

"Yes, an' how are we goin' to get hold of the plans?" said Ginger.

"Well, we'll have to think that out a bit," said William. "I'll have a good practice at black magic signs tonight an' tomorrow we'll have a go at gettin' the plans."

They met in the old barn the next day and William

brought two crumpled sheets of paper from his pocket.

"I tore them out of the middle of my arithmetic exercise book," he said.

"You did that for the paper boats last week," said Henry.

"Yes, but it's not got thin enough for Frenchie to notice yet," said William. "Look!" He unfolded the paper and held it out. "There they are! They're jolly good, aren't they? Red ink gives 'em a specially *evil* look, doesn't it? This one's pretty awful, isn't it? An' this one—the one that's puttin' its tongue out—it jus' breathes evil, doesn't it?"

"They look more like cats to me," said Ginger.

"This one has a sort of a look of a tortoise," said Douglas.

"They're jolly good black magic signs," said William indignantly. "They'd scare anyone to death. . . . Well, now we've got to get those plans."

"We don't know where he keeps them," said Ginger.

"Well, we can find out, can't we?" said William. "They must be somewhere in his house. We'll go round to his house an' wait till we get a chance then we'll slip into his house an' find the plans an' put black magic signs on them an'—an' he'll be so scared he won't build a single house."

"Sounds all right," said Ginger.

"There's laws against goin' into people's houses," said Douglas, "an' I bet there's laws against puttin' black magic signs on people's plans."

"All right," said William. "If you'd rather never see the old barn again an' have houses built all over our fields, don't come, then."

But he came. The four of them made their way again

over the fields to Ivy Lodge. It was just as they were approaching the house that they saw the figure of the architect emerge from the gate and set off down the road in the opposite direction. He wore a dark city suit and carried a brief case.

"I bet he's goin' to London," said William, drawing his gang back into the shelter of the hedge. "Wait till he's out of sight."

They waited till he was out of sight, then cautiously approached the ivy-covered house and stood in the gateway, surveying the premises. The garden was empty. The house wore a vaguely unoccupied look.

"Let's go round to the back," said William. "I bet no one's in. If someone is, we'll say we've lost our way or ask for a drink of water."

They followed him round the side of the house then stopped short. At the back of the house was a paved terrace from which a short flight of steps led down to the lawn, and on the bottom step a little girl was sitting. A long plait hung down each shoulder and he head was bent over a book. She looked up at the sound of the Outlaws' footsteps. William had made a movement of retreat but it was too late.

"What do you want?" she said.

William approached her with a nonchalant swagger.

"Nothin'," he said. "Well, nothin' much. I mean, would you like to do somethin' to save the countryside?"

"No, thank you," said the little girl and bent her head over her book again.

William decided to try a more personal approach.

"What's your name?" he said.

"Fenella."

"An'—an' that architect man's your father?"

"No. He's my grandfather. I'm staying with him while

my mother and father are abroad." A warmer note had come into her voice. She was not interested in the Outlaws or their activities, but she was definitely interested in herself and her situation. "I'm going to stay with an aunt next week and then I'm coming back here to my grandfather till my mother and father come home."

"Your grandfather *is* an architect, isn't he?" said Henry.

"Oh, yes, he's a marvellous architect."

"And he draws plans for houses, doesn't he?"

"Oh, yes, he draws marvellous plans."

"He's drawing some now, isn't he?"

"He's drawing one."

"Only one?" said Henry. "I thought——"

" 'Course he'd only draw one to start with," said William. "It'd be a sort of pattern an' he'd do the others like it." He turned to the little girl. "I bet you don't know where he keeps this plan."

"Yes, I do," said Fenella. "He doesn't know I do. He doesn't know I know anything about it, but I found it in a drawer in his desk this morning, so I *do* know."

"I bet you're makin' it up," said William.

"I'm not," said the little girl indignantly. "I *saw* it."

"All right. Show it us."

"Yes, I will."

She sprang to her feet and entered the house by the french window, returning a few moments later with a piece of paper that she held tantalisingly out of the Outlaws' reach. It was obviously a "blue print", and on it the plan of a house was clearly outlined, with rooms and measurements complete.

"Lend it us," said William persuasively.

"No," said Fenella.

She went into the house again and returned without the plan.

"Lend it us jus' for half an hour," pleaded William.

Fenella sat down on the bottom step and fixed a brightly speculative eye on him.

"What will you give me if I do?" she said.

"Gosh!" said William. "Won't you do a little thing like lendin' a plan to save the countryside for nothin'?"

"No," said Fenella.

"I'll give you an ice lolly," said Ginger.

"No," said Fenella.

"A jigsaw of Buckingham Palace with only two pieces missing," said Henry, adding, "well, maybe three."

"No," said Fenella.

"A joke spider," said Douglas. "Jus' like a real one. Put it on someone's pillow an' they go right up in the air."

"No," said Fenella.

"Well, what *do* you want?" said William.

"A donkey," said Fenella.

William gasped.

"A *what*?"

"A donkey," repeated Fenella. She took up the book she had been reading. "The little girls in this book have got a donkey. It's a book called *Flat Iron for a Farthing* and the little girls in it have got a donkey, so I want one, too. If you'll give me a donkey, I'll get the plan for you."

"We haven't *got* a donkey to give you," said William. "Listen! I'll give you a ring I got out of a cracker at Christmas with an emerald in. A *huge* emerald. It's so huge it *mus'* be valu'ble. That's why I kept it."

"I don't want anything but a donkey," said Fenella firmly. "If you won't give me a donkey you can go away."

70

"All right, we jolly well *will* go away," said William. He walked to the side of the house, followed by the other three. At the side of the house he turned and spoke with dignity. "An' we'll come back with a donkey."

"Gosh, William!" said Ginger when they reached the road. "Why did you say that? We can't poss'bly find a donkey."

"We've *got* to," said William grimly. "If we don't want houses all over our fields an' the old barn gone for ever, we've got to get a donkey."

"How?" said Douglas.

"Oh, stop askin' silly questions," said William irritably. "When ever I get a really smashin' plan you all start makin' objections. There mus' *be* donkeys, mustn't there? We mus' be able to find one *somewhere*. We'll jus' walk along till we see one."

"Well, we know all the places round here," said Henry, "an' we know there isn't a donkey in any of them."

"We've not been to Applelea for weeks," said William thoughtfully. "Let's go over there. Anythin' might have happened since we were there last."

"There's plenty of cows about," said Henry gloomily, as they walked over the fields.

"An' sheep," said Ginger.

"There's caterpillars, too," said Douglas. "Why did she have to pick on a donkey?"

"Come to think of it," said Ginger, "it's ages since I saw a donkey. They're prob'ly died out, same as dinosaurs."

They walked through the village of Applelea, throwing searching glances at the fields and gardens as they passed.

"We'll have to give it up," said Henry at last. "Fate isn't on our side."

"All right," said William. "We'll jus' go to where the

lane turns round an' if there isn't anythin' there we'll go back. . . . Gosh!" he added regretfully. "They were wizard black magic signs. They'd have scared him into fits."

Slowly, dejectedly, they walked to the end of the lane. And there they stopped and stood in silence, paralysed by amazement. For, from the gate of a cottage by the side of the lane, a donkey was emerging at a brisk trot. An old woman was accelerating its progress from behind with a stick.

"Off with you!" she said. "And don't come back or I'll give you what for! Off you go! And don't let me ever see you here again."

She closed the gate and returned to the cottage, slamming the door.

"Gosh!" breathed William. "A *donkey*!"

"Fate *is* on our side," said Henry

The donkey looked up and down the lane, then began to approach the Outlaws in a slow and tentative fashion.

"Good ole donkey!" William encouraged it.

"Come on! Good ole donkey!" said Ginger.

"Good boy! Good ole boy!" said Douglas.

The donkey raised its voice in a raucous "hee haw" and Douglas retreated hastily towards the hedge.

"Well, we wanted a donkey an' we've got one," said William triumphantly.

"It's not ours, you know," said Henry. "You can't just *take* donkeys."

"Well, it belonged to that old woman," said William, "an' she didn't want it. She *said* so."

"I wonder why she didn't want it," said Ginger. "There's nothin' wrong with it. It looks a perfectly good donkey."

The donkey flapped its ears as if in agreement. It seemed to be waiting anxiously for their decision.

"Tell you what it might be," said William. "There was somethin' about it in a paper I was readin' las' Sat'day. Sometimes people that are goin' away for their holiday and haven't anywhere to leave their pets jus' turn 'em out to starve an' it's jolly unkind an' I bet that's what the old woman was doin'. This donkey was her pet an' she was goin' away for a holiday an' she hadn't anywhere to leave it so she was turnin' it out to starve. She was sendin' it out with a stick an' tellin' it not to come back, so it *mus'* have been that."

"What did this paper say you'd got to do if you found one?" said Henry.

"It said if you were sure it'd been turned out to starve it would be an act of kindness to give it a home. Well, we're sure this one's been turned out to starve 'cause we saw her doin' it so now it b'longs to us an' we can take it to that girl to give it a home, an' get the plans of the house an' put the black magic signs on it an' scare that man so's he won't build the houses an' everythin' will be all right."

The others considered the situation in silence for some moments. The donkey looked at them inquiringly, jerking one ear forward and the other backward.

"It's a jolly fine donkey," said William proudly.

"Funny sort of colour," said Ginger.

"Brown," said Douglas.

"Not quite," said William.

"Sandy," said Henry.

"That's a good name," said William. "We'll call him Sandy. . . . Come on, Sandy. . . . Come on, ole boy. I'm goin' to have a ride on him. Help me up."

They helped him up. He sat astride Sandy for a few fleeting seconds . . . then Sandy kicked up his heels in a sudden unexpected movement and he went head over heels into the air, landing on the ground a few feet away.

"Let me have a try," said Ginger.

He had a try and landed on the road beside William.

They picked themselves up and stood rubbing their bruises, eyeing Sandy a little apprehensively Sandy waved his tail, waggled his ears and began to crop the grass by the roadside.

"He evidently isn't the sort you ride," said William. "Pity we've not got a piece of rope to pull him along."

"There's his tail an' his ears," said Ginger.

"He's watchin' us," said Henry.

Sandy was throwing wicked sidelong glances at them as he ate.

"He's plottin' somethin'," said Douglas.

"We'll jus' have to *coax* him along," said William. He advanced towards the donkey. "Come on, Sandy! Good ole Sandy!"

"We may have to pull him backwards by his tail," said Henry.

"We'll try a bit more coaxin' first," said William.

Suddenly Sandy tossed his head and set off at a brisk run down the lane, scattering the Outlaws headlong in his flight.

"Come on," said William, scrambling to his feet. "Let's catch him."

They ran down the lane to the road and looked up and down. . . . Nothing was in sight.

"Look! There he is!" shouted William.

Sandy's head could just be seen over a distant hedge. He had crossed the road and was careering down a lane on the other side. They followed. . . . Sandy was nimbler than he looked. He led them down every lane and by-way that offered itself . . . then suddenly, when they thought that they had completely lost track of him, they came upon him standing decorously by the roadside, nibbling the lower branches of a beech tree. He waggled his ears in sign of greeting and trotted daintily towards them.

"Gosh! He's brought us nearly back home," said William. "We'll have an awful time gettin' him to Marleigh."

Their progress to Marleigh was as erratic as William had foreseen. Sandy seemed to be a creature of moods, of sudden spurts of gaiety, of long spells of silent thought. He would canter briskly down the road, then stand motionless. They pulled and pushed and prodded, but he refused to move till again the sudden spurt of gaiety came over him. Once he lay down by the roadside and appeared to be composing himself to sleep when some impulse made him spring to his feet without warning and canter briskly in the direction from which they had come.

"I'm jus' about worn out," said Douglas at last. "Let's give it up."

"No, we won't," said William doggedly. "We said we'd get her a donkey an' we *will*. Anyway, we've got to stop 'em buildin' those houses, haven't we? It's worth takin' a bit of trouble over, isn't it?"

"A *bit* of trouble!" echoed Douglas with an ironic laugh.

"We'd better get him along quick," said Henry. "We're jus' passin' Miss Milton's house an' she'll make an awful fuss if he starts anythin' here."

Anxiously they approached Miss Milton's house. Sandy stopped at the gate and looked at it with interest.

"Catch hold of his tail," said William urgently.

Ginger caught hold of his tail, but, with a deft flick, Sandy freed himself and they watched helplessly as he trotted up the short path and in at the open front door.

75

"Gosh!" said William. "I hope he doesn't do any damage."

His hopes were short-lived. There came the sound of the breaking of crockery, followed by a piercing scream in Miss Milton's well-known voice. Then Sandy, having kicked over the tea table in the sitting-room, came frisking out by way of the french window, obviously in fine fettle and highly pleased with himself.

"Let's get away quick," said William.

They hurried on down the lane. A group of wide-eyed village children, who had watched the proceedings with interest, followed slowly. Sandy led the way, trotting in a prim decorous fashion . . . then suddenly he disappeared through another gateway.

"Gosh! Where's he gone now?" said William.

Fearfully they approached the gate. In the short driveway General Moult was cleaning his car. He had recently bought a new gadget for cleaning his car. A bucket of water stood on the roof of his car and from it descended a hose pipe with which the General was spraying the paint work. His back was turned to Sandy and he was unaware of Sandy's presence till he received the playful butt in the back that brought the bucket on to his head. He sat down abruptly, the bucket covering his face, the water pouring around him. His bellow of rage was muffled but penetrating. It obviously startled Sandy, who uttered his raucous "hee haw", then went trotting down the drive to join the Outlaws.

"We can't go on like this," said Henry. "We'll have to let it go."

"All right," said William despondently.

Even William felt that he was beaten.

They hurried on down the road. But Sandy had no intention of losing his new friends. He followed closely on their heels, nuzzling William's neck when William turned round to shoo him off.

"Let's hurry on an' not turn round," said William.

They hurried on . . but turned round sharply as a sudden clatter came from behind them. They had not noticed the small greengrocer's handcart by the roadside, but it had not escaped Sandy's notice. Sandy had already grabbed a bunch of small carrots from it. scattering lettuces and cabbages on to the road in the process. The greengrocer emerged from the gate with a shout of anger, and Sandy, kicking up his heels and shaking the bunch of carrots playfully in his mouth, dodged round the cart and turned on down the road after the Outlaws.

"Let's go into the field an' get away from him," said Henry.

They climbed the stile into the field and set off quickly. But they soon realised that Sandy was still close on their heels. He could not manage the stile, but he had found a convenient opening in the hedge and was trotting along behind them, munching his bunch of carrots.

"Oh, well," said William, "we're nearly at Marleigh now, so we'll give him to that girl an' get the plan an' put the black magic signs on it an' everything'll be all right."

"I wonder!" said Douglas dolefully.

Sandy seemed anxious to atone for his irresponsible conduct. Beyond taking a tentative mouthful of Ginger's blazer and rejecting it as uneatable, and chasing a cow round a haystack, he followed them docilely enough till they reached the gateway of Ivy Lodge.

"We've got to make him behave prop'ly, so she'll want to keep him," said William. "Come on, Sandy. Come on, Sandy, ole boy."

Ginger took hold of the tail and Henry and Douglas

each took hold of an ear and William walked in front, stretching out his arms to regulate the pace of the procession. Slowly they walked round the side of the house to the back garden. The little girl was still sitting on the step reading her book.

"Well, we've brought you the donkey," said William, "an' now p'raps you'll let us have those plans of the house."

Suddenly the architect walked out of the open french window.

"Hello, hello, hello," he said. "What's all this?"

William threw a horror-stricken glance around and decided to yield to the inevitable.

"She wanted a donkey," he said, "an' we said we'd get her a donkey if she'd give us those plans, so we've got her a donkey same as we said."

"What plans?" said the architect.

"The plans of those houses you're goin' to build."

The architect looked puzzled.

"I'm not going to build any houses," he said.

"Yes, you are," said William sternly. "I saw you measurin' an' she showed us one of the plans."

"It's in the top drawer of your desk," said Fenella. "I found it this morning and showed it to them and it *is* a plan of a house."

"You little monkey!" said the architect. "It was meant to be a secret."

"Funny sort of secret!" said William. "Buildin' houses all over the place!"

"I don't know what you're talking about," said Mr. Anderson. "My little granddaughter is going away next week to stay with one of her aunts and I'd planned to make a Wendy house for her in the garden as a surprise for her on her return. Perhaps you'll kindly explain how

78

"Well, we've brought you the donkey," said William.

the donkey comes into it. Also, if you've any control over it perhaps you'll kindly stop it eating geraniums out of that tub."

Henry pulled Sandy by his tail out of the geranium tub. Sandy kicked up his heels then lay down on the lawn, looking bored, resigned and slightly contemptuous.

"B-but," said William. "But you are an architect an' you made the plans for a house . . ."

"Oh, yes, I'm an architect," said Mr. Anderson, "but I'm not in practice any longer. I retired, you see, last year. As to the plan . . . though it was only a child's garden house, the habit of years was too strong for me and I couldn't help making a real job of it—all drawn to scale in my best professional manner. I meant it to be a secret, but evidently the little monkey dug it out. But why, may I ask you, *why* did you want it?"

"Because I saw you," said William, "measurin' out that field by the old barn an' countin' how many houses you could get into it. I *saw* you."

Enlightenment shone suddenly in Mr. Anderson's face.

"Oh, that!" he said. "Good Heavens! I see now. No, I'm on the committee for arranging the gala in celebration of the centenary of the granting of Hadley's charter."

William stared at him in bewilderment.

"You see, my boy," said Mr. Anderson patiently. "In the old days, Hadley was just a little village like Marleigh and Applelea and the others, but a hundred years ago it became clear that it had grown into a small town, and it was granted a charter so that it could become a borough with a Borough Council and all the rest of it. Anyway, we thought we'd have some high jinks to celebrate it and they put me on the committee for a Grand Gala to be held in those fields with marquees and competitions and stalls and coconut-shies and what-not. I was measuring up the space for the marquees and stalls to see how many we could get into it "

"Oh . . ." said William. "So no one's goin' to build houses in those fields?"

"Good Lord, no! There's no fear of that. But I still don't see where the donkey comes into it."

They looked at the donkey. Sandy still lay on the lawn and Fenella sat by him, encircling his neck with her arm, leaning her cheek against his ear. Sandy's face seemed to wear a pleased and sheepish expression.

"Well, it was like this . . ." began William.

His story was not very coherent—interspersed, as it was, by comments from the other three—but apparently Mr. Anderson gathered the gist of it. He gave a shout of laughter.

"I wish I hadn't come home till later. I'd like to have seen the black magic signs."

"They were pretty awful," said William solemnly.

"But—who does the donkey belong to?"

"Oh, it's ours all right," said William. "We found someone turnin' it out to starve 'cause they were goin' on a holiday, so we took it to give it a good home."

"Yes, but——" began Mr. Anderson. "Hello! Who's this?"

A little old man was coming round the side of the house. He had a small wizened face and bright blue eyes. His face broke into a smile when he saw Sandy.

"There you are, you little rascal!" he chuckled. "A fine dance you've led me and no mistake!"

"Now let's get to the bottom of this," said Mr. Anderson. "Whose *is* this donkey?"

" 'E's mine, sir," said the old man. "Best donkey in the land, 'e is, but I've 'ad to go and live with my son over at Applelea. Couldn't do for myself no longer 'cause of my rheumatics. An' Neddy here came with me. But there's no room at my son's for Neddy. 'E gets out and wanders." He chuckled again. " 'E was always a one for wanderin'. In an' out of people's gardens all over the place. Old Mrs. Abbott gets proper mad at 'im. Seems 'e's always after her lettuces. She says she turned 'im out this mornin'. At first I couldn't think where 'e'd gone then I 'eard of 'im gallivantin' off with them four boys."

"We thought he was a stray," said William.

"He acted like one," said Ginger.

" 'E does," said the old man with another chuckle. "it's 'is fun. 'E's got a wonnerful sense of fun." His face clouded over. "I'll 'ave to get rid of 'im, though. I can't keep 'im at my son's no longer. It's not fair to either of them." He sighed. "We've been through some times together, Neddy an' me. Before my rheumatics got bad I used to take 'im round to fairs an' fêtes an' suchlike, givin' rides to kiddies. I've still got the saddle. Back-to-back they used to sit on it."

"Like the one in my book," said Fenella.

"Ha!" ejaculated Mr. Anderson. "Just what I wanted. I've arranged races and competitions for the older children, but I wanted something for the toddlers. Donkey Rides for Toddlers! Just the thing! Will you come with Neddy and the saddle and give donkey rides for toddlers at the Gala?"

The old man grinned.

"Sure I will," he said.

"But what about me?" wailed Fenella. "It was going to be *my* donkey and now it's everybody's donkey but mine."

"Why didn't you tell me you wanted a donkey, my dear?" said Mr. Anderson.

"I didn't know till I'd read the book."

"Well, well, well," said Mr. Anderson. He turned to the old man. "Did you say you couldn't keep the donkey at your son's?"

" 'Fraid so, sir. My son's sorry about it, too, but there it is!"

"If you're thinking of selling him," said Mr. Anderson, "may I buy him for my granddaughter? You can come and see him whenever you like. There's a paddock at the end of the garden. I think he'll be happy. You must teach the child to ride him and look after him. Will you agree to that?"

The little man's face shone with pleasure.

"Indeed I will, sir, and it's an 'eavy load off my mind, it is indeed. I couldn't bear the thought of sendin' 'im to strangers."

"Well, we're not strangers," said Mr. Anderson, "and you'll see lots of him." The sound of voices reached them growing nearer and clearer. "Now who on earth are these?"

William had recognised the voices. He peeped round the side of the house. Miss Milton and General Moult had reached the gate. . . . A short distance behind them came the greengrocer. It was plain that the little group of wide-eyed children had followed the Outlaws to Ivy Lodge and lost no time in informing Miss Milton and General Moult of their whereabouts.

"Gosh!" said William aghast. "It's Miss Milton an' General Moult an' the man with the cart. . . . The donkey knocked over her tea-table an' brought down a bucket of water on his head an' took carrots off the other one's cart an' they'll all say it was our fault an'——"

Mr. Anderson had grasped the situation.

"I'll make it all right with them," he said. "I'm more than grateful to you for providing a donkey for my toddlers *and* for my granddaughter. Don't worry. I'll make it all right with them. But you'd better go while the going's good. The green gate at the bottom of the garden leads to the paddock, you can slip out by that."

Dazedly, huddling together, keeping in the shadow of the hedge, they made their way to the green gate, quickening their footsteps as the sound of Miss Milton's high-pitched voice floated out from the french window. They crossed the paddock and reached the road. There they stopped to rally their forces.

"I thought things were never goin' to stop happenin'," said Henry.

"They never did," said William.

"What'll we do now?" said Douglas.

"I'm jus' about worn out," said Ginger. "Let's go somewhere we can get a bit of peace."

William drew a long deep sigh.

"Let's go to the old barn," he said.

CHAPTER IV

DOUGLAS'S GREAT EXPERIENCE

WILLIAM climbed over the stile and made his way slowly across the fields to the old barn. His brow was furrowed, his expression one of deep and anxious thought. Ginger and Henry were waiting for him in the doorway. He threw a quick glance round the interior of the barn.

"He's not come?" he said.

"No," said Henry gloomily.

"An' he didn't come yesterday," said William.

"He was goin' to come yesterday," said Ginger, "but she fetched him to set out her toy farm."

"He needn't have gone if he hadn't wanted to," said William with a hint of sternness in his voice.

"He did want to," said Henry. "That's the worst of it, him *wantin'* to do these awful things."

"An' he went to tea with her the day before yesterday," said Ginger.

"An' to a picnic with her the day before that," said Henry.

"An' he'd promised to go to the woods with us on Tuesday for Cowboys an' Indians," said William, "an' he didn't turn up jus' 'cause she wanted him to fix her dolls' house roof for her."

"An' he's been playin' 'Mothers an' Fathers' with her," said Henry, disgustedly.

"It makes you *sick*," said Ginger.

"He's not been out with us for days," said Henry.

"An' *Douglas*!" said William. "Douglas, that never knew what to do without us till now!"

For Douglas had fallen a victim to the charms of a little girl called Patsy Willingham who lived with her parents in a square Victorian house on the outskirts of the village, and he now spent most of his time hanging round the gates, waiting for invitations, performing menial tasks and accompanying the jaunty little figure of Patsy on all its comings and goings.

"He's turned into a sort of *slave*," said William bitterly. "He doesn't seem *yuman* any longer. It makes you feel sort of—sort of——"

"Ashamed for him," said Henry.

"Yes, that's it," said William. "Ashamed for him. An' he was quite decent before this happened."

"You jus' wouldn't think it *could* have happened," said Ginger.

"It's happened before in hist'ry," said Henry. "It happened to Anthony an' Cleopatra. She—she got him right down same as Patsy's got Douglas an' that was the end of him."

"What was the end?" said William.

"He killed himself an' she got stung by a snake."

"That's jolly serious," said William. "We don't want that sort of thing to happen to ole Douglas."

"An' there was a man called Dant in hist'ry, too," said Henry, "that got a crush on a girl called Beatrice, but he lived a long way away from her so he couldn't see much of her so he jus' wrote poems instead."

"Well, that wouldn't have been so bad," said William. She couldn't have been always draggin' him off to mend her dolls' house or set out her toy farm or play awful games with her."

"Look!" said Ginger. "He's comin'."

Douglas could be seen coming across the field from the stile. His face was downcast, his hands thrust deep into his pockets. He trailed his feet over the grass as he walked. He didn't raise his eyes until he reached the door of the barn and then he raised them slowly to the three stern accusing faces.

"I can't come with you today," he said. "Patsy's got a new tricycle an' she wants me to help her learn to ride it."

There was a mixture of defiance and sheepishness in his voice.

"An' you didn't come yesterday or the day before that," said William.

"I know," said Douglas. "I—I can't help it."

"You don't try," said William severely.

86

"I do try. I can't help it "

"Why don't you jus' write po'try same as Dant an' not keep on goin' to see her?"

"I can't write po'try," said Douglas, "an'—an' I can't help goin' to see her."

They stood in the doorway watching him as he trailed back across the field

"Why can't you help goin' to see her?" said Henry.

"I don't know," said Douglas. "I can't explain. It's—it's somethin' about her face."

"Well, she's only got an ordin'ry face with a nose an' two eyes an' a mouth," said William. "It's no diff'rent from anyone else's."

"It *is* diff'rent," said Douglas. "I can't explain but it *is* diff'rent."

They looked at him, gravely concerned, as if they were doctors, considering a serious medical case.

"You've been like this for over a week, you know," said William.

"I know," said Douglas helplessly.

"Doesn't it get any better?" said Ginger.

"It doesn't seem to," said Douglas. He fidgeted uneasily. "Well, I'd better go now. I don't want to keep her waitin'."

They stood in the doorway watching him as he trailed back across the field. Once in the road, he seemed to shed his gloom and began to run almost eagerly in the direction of Patsy's home.

"I'm sorry for him in a way," said Henry, as they turned back towards the interior of the barn.

"Yes, but it's jolly serious," said William. "We've got to do somethin' about it."

"It might wear off," said Ginger. "P'raps if we leave it alone it'll wear off."

"It might take *weeks*," said William. "I think we ought to do somethin' now to save him from himself."

"It's the horns of a dilemma," said Henry. "To do somethin' now to save him from himself or wait till it wears off."

"Let's toss for it," said Ginger.

"Anyone got a penny?" said William.

No one had.

"Well, I think tossin' up's a silly way of doin' it, anyway," said William. "They fall heads an' then they roll over an' end up tails an' you don't know which they meant. Let's think of another way."

"The ancient Romans did it by animals somehow," said Henry vaguely.

"How?" said William.

"I'm not sure," said Henry. "I've forgotten."

"Animals . . ." said William. He went to the doorway of the barn. "Cows. . . There's cows in the next field. We could do it by cows. . . . *Tell* you what! We'll count the cows in the next field an' if it's an odd number we'll wait for it to wear off an' if it's an even number we'll *do* somethin' about it."

The others agreed. They stood by the hedge and counted . . . eight cows. They counted again. It was still eight cows.

"So we've got to *do* somethin' to save him from himself," said William. There was a note of satisfaction in his voice. Policies of inaction never appealed to William. "Come on. Let's think what to do."

They sat down on the grass in the doorway of the old barn and remained for some moments in silent thought.

"We might get 'em to remove somehow," said Ginger at last.

"How?" challenged William.

"Well . . . haunt the house. Make them think it's got a ghost. Then p'raps they'd go."

"We've tried hauntin' houses," said William, "an' it wasn't any good."

There was another long silence, then:

"*Tell* you what!" said William.

"Yes?"

"Well, you know what Douglas is like He's always scared of doin' things against the law. Trespassin' an' suchlike. Well, if we can make him think this girl's father's a crim'nal, it'll scare him right off."

"Or her mother . . ." said Ginger.

They considered Patsy's parents. Mr. Willingham was a tall thick-set man with so prolific a growth of eyebrow, moustache and beard that the Outlaws had nicknamed him "Bushy". Mrs. Willingham was small and vague and placid.

"Her mother *couldn't* be made to seem like a crim'nal," said William, "but her father could. . . . He looks exactly like a crim'nal. I bet we could easy fix somethin' he did to look like a crime an' scare Douglas off."

"How'll we do it?" said Ginger.

"We'll have to watch him," said William. "Shadow him an' dog his footsteps same as detectives. We'll have to get hold of somethin' quite ordin'ry he does an' pile it on a bit an' make out it's against the law an' scare ole Douglas off with it."

"I bet it won't be as easy as that," said Henry.

"I bet it will," said William, "an' even if it isn't we've got to save Douglas from himself, haven't we? An' it's worth takin' a bit of trouble over, isn't it?"

"When do we start doggin' his footsteps?" said Henry.

"Today," said William. "There's no time to waste. It's *desp'rate*, with Douglas gettin' worse an' worse every minute. We've *got* to do somethin' to save him from himself."

"D'you mean, start this very minute?" said Ginger.

"We'll wait till ole Bushy gets back from London. He works on a newspaper there every day an' I think he gets back about six. So we'll meet outside his house. . . . What's it called?"

"Roxborough," said Henry.

"Yes, Roxborough. Well, we'll meet outside it about six an' start doggin' his footsteps."

The three met at six o'clock and took up their positions on the opposite side of the road from Roxborough, keeping in the shadow of the hedge that grew by the roadside. Roxborough had an air of solid respectability, with a porticoed doorway and a laurel-bordered drive. A lane ran between it and the next house, Elm Mead. Elm Mead wore a dejected, defeated air. A notice "For Sale" stood behind an overgrown hedge.

He stood there for a few moments, throwing furtive glances up and down the road.

"That's been empty for ages," said Henry. "It's where the Harts used to live."

"I expect ole Bushy's usin' it for the headquarters of his gang," said William, who was now firmly convinced of Mr. Willingham's criminal activities. "He prob'ly keeps all his smash-an'-grab stuff hidden there."

91

"He's not really a crim'nal," Henry reminded him. "He's jus' an ordin'ry respectable citizen. We're only goin' to make *out* he's a crim'nal to save Douglas from himself."

"We may be runnin' into somethin' bigger than we think," said William darkly. "There's lots of crim'nals goin' about disguised as ordin'ry respectable citizens."

"Look!" said Ginger. "There he is! That's his car."

A blue-grey car was coming slowly down the road. It stopped at the gate of Elm Mead.

"Why's he stoppin' there?" said Henry. "That's not his house."

"Let's watch him," said William. "He—— *Gosh!*"

For Mr. Willingham had got out of the car and taken from it a large square parcel wrapped apparently in cardboard. He stood there for a few moments, throwing furtive glances up and down the road, then, keeping in the shadow of the bushes, made his way up the short drive of Elm Mead. The boys watched as he opened the garage door, disappeared for a few moments inside, then reappeared without the parcel. He walked down the drive in the same furtive manner, entered his car again, and drove in at the gate of Roxborough.

"Gosh!" said William. "He *is* a crim'nal. He's a thief and he's hidin' the things he steals in that empty garage. He's got some things he's stolen in that parcel. He's prob'ly robbed a bank today."

"It's not big enough for a bank," said Henry.

"Well, diamonds or furs or bullion or secret plans or foreign stamps or drugs or somethin'," said William. "Anyway, it was somethin' he'd got to *hide* He's a crook all right. . . . Come on. Let's see what it was "

"We won't be able to get into the garage."

"Yes, we will. That lock doesn't work prop'ly. You

give the door a good hard push an' it slips open. Mrs. Hart used to do it. I've often helped her . . . . Come along. An' don't make a sound. We don't want him to know we're on his tracks. He'd stick at nothin' if he found out."

Silently, heads bent between hunched shoulders, they made their way across the road, in at the gate of Elm Mead, and up to the garage. William gave the doors a quick hard push and they opened. The boys entered. The garage was empty except for the parcel they had seen Mr. Willingham carrying into it. It bore large red labels: HIGHLY INFLAMMABLE. DANGEROUS. HANDLE WITH CARE.

"It's a bomb," said William with quiet conviction.

"What's he put it there for?" said Henry

"Well, he couldn't put it in his own house. Prob'ly his wife doesn't know anythin' about his life of crime an' anyway he doesn't want to get his own house blown up."

"What's he goin' to do with it?"

"He's prob'ly a secret agent," said William, "an' he's goin' to throw it into a public meetin' or put it in a plane. Why, you read in the papers every day about people throwin' bombs in public meetin's or puttin' them in planes. Or—*tell* you what! He's prob'ly goin' to use it to wreck that newspaper place he works in. You see, if he blew up all the newspapers there wouldn't be any newspapers an' no one would know what was happenin' an' he could seize power an' rule the country. That's what he's tryin' to do. He's startin' with his own paper then he'll go on and blow up all the others."

"P'raps we'd better leave it alone," said Ginger.

"Gosh, we can't do that," said William indignantly. "Not with a *bomb*! It might go off any minute an' kill people for miles round. We've got to *do* somethin' about it."

"Well, what can we do?" said Ginger.

93

"Put it in water," said William. "I've read about people doin' that with bombs. Come on. Let's put it in water."

"How?" said Ginger.

"Where?" said Henry.

William looked round the empty garage.

"There doesn't seem to be any water here," he said. "There's taps in some garages but there isn't here. Let's go into the house. We can get into the house by that door. It goes into the passage an' into the kitchen. Ole Bushy keeps the keys but Douglas an' that girl have been playin' here, so I bet the kitchen door's not locked."

The kitchen door wasn't locked. They entered the kitchen, William holding the parcel at arm's length, his head turned aside.

"I don't want it goin' off right into my face," he explained. "Turn on the tap, Ginger."

Ginger turned on the tap. No water came.

"They've turned it off at the main," said Henry. "They do that in empty houses 'case of frost."

"They might have the sense to leave it on 'case of bombs," said William severely. "We'll have to try the bathroom."

They tried the bathroom. Still no water came.

"I think we'd better give it up," said Ginger.

"Well, I'm jolly well not goin' to give it up," said William testily. "I've started it an' I'm not goin' to give it up. I'm goin' to find some water *somehow*. I'm. . . . Gosh! There mus' be some in the tank. I know there's a tank in the loft. Come on. Let's try."

They walked along the empty dust-covered landing, their footsteps echoing on the bare wood-n floor.

"Yes, it's up there," said William, stopping to look up at a small trapdoor in the ceiling. "An' the ladder's in that little room there."

94

Ginger fetched the ladder and set it up against the trapdoor. Slowly they ascended, William clasping his parcel with one hand and pulling himself up with the other. They stood in the loft and looked at the galvanised iron tank that occupied most of the room. It was boarded over.

"I 'spect they've done it to keep flies an' things out," said Henry.

"I don't care why they've done it," said William. "Let's get it off."

They struggled with it unavailingly for some minutes, then William set the parcel on the top of the boarded tank and considered the situation.

"We could take it to the pond," he said.

"Or the river," said Henry.

"Or there's Miss Thompson's garden pool," said Ginger, "but it'd give her goldfish a bit of a shock if it went off there."

"Anyway, let's get it down again," said William. "It's no good stayin' up here. Every minute's precious with things like bombs. I don't even know whether I'm holdin' in the right way up. You go first, Ginger."

And then the catastrophe happened. For Ginger, trying to straighten the end of the ladder that rested on the open trapdoor, lost grip on it . . . and it fell with a resounding clatter on to the wooden floor beneath.

"You *clot*, Ginger!" said William.

"I'm sorry," gasped Ginger. "It sort of slithered out of my hand."

The three anxious faces peered down through the twelve feet of space.

"It's no good tryin' to jump," said William. "If we've got to choose between breakin' our necks an' bein' killed by a bomb, I'd sooner be killed by a bomb. I don't want

to go about for the rest of my life with a broken neck."
He dropped the trapdoor into place. "Might as well shut
it, then we won't be fallin' down it by mistake."

They stood round the tank, gazing at the parcel. Something of William's ruddy colour had faded.

"Gosh!" he said. "Here we are imprisoned for life with
a bomb!"

"An' it mightn't be a long one," said Henry. "Life,
I mean."

"When will it go off?" said Ginger.

"Any time," said William. "You can't tell with bombs.
An' even if it doesn't go off, we might be here for
months without anyone findin' us. It's such a rotten old
house, hardly anyone comes to look at it. We might be
dead of starvation before anyone found us."

Ginger blinked.

"How long does it take to die of starvation?" he said.

"I dunno," said Henry. "I believe it's a long, slow
death. Anyway, the bomb'll prob'ly go off before then.
. . . Gosh! There's lots of things I'd have done if I'd
known this was going to happen. I'd have finished that
space-ship model so that people would have had somethin'
to remember me by."

"An' I'd have tried that experiment of makin' a magnet
out of a penknife," said Ginger. "I'll never know now
whether it would have come off or not."

"Well, if you'd known this was goin to happen," said
William, "you wouldn' have come here, an' it wouldn't
have happened, an' if it hadn't happened you couldn't
have known it was goin' to happen 'cause it wasn't goin'
to happen so——" A moment's consideration convinced
him that he was getting out of his depths and he returned
to the immediate problem. "Anyway, let's *do* somethin'.
There must be some way of gettin' out." His eyes scanned

96

*William gazed through the aperture. "We could
get out on to the roof . . ."*

D

the ceiling and came to rest on a cobweb-covered skylight just above the tank. "Let's try that . . ."

Cautiously he removed the parcel to the floor and climbed on to the tank. With a creaking, grating noise the skylight slowly opened. William gazed through the aperture.

"We could get out on to the roof . . ."

"That doesn't take us any nearer the ground," said Ginger, "an' if that bomb does go off it'll be as likely to get us on the roof as anywhere else."

"I dunno," said Henry doubtfully. "There's the force of gravity . . ."

"Oh, come on," said William. "Let's get out of here."

Led by William, they swung themselves up through the open skylight on to the roof. The roof was a flat one, bordered by a low parapet. They went to the parapet and gazed over it. Through the trees they could see into the garden of Roxborough and the lane that ran between the two houses.

"Gosh! Look at ole Douglas," said William, "pushin' her round the lawn on a tricycle. It's about time we saved him from himself."

"An' there's ole Bushy," said Henry, "walkin' down the lane."

They craned their necks to look over the parapet.

Mr. Willingham could be seen at the farther end of the lane. He was walking in a stumbling uncertain fashion.

"He's walkin' as if he was blind." said William.

"He's got his eyes shut," said Ginger.

"He's opened them now . ."

"He's *seen* us. He's lookin' straight at us."

"He's turned round. . . . He's goin' back the way he came."

"He's goin' pretty quick, too. He's nearly runnin'."

"He knows we're on his track," said William. "He knows we've found his bomb. He's gone to get a deadly weapon against us."

"Or round up his gang of crim'nals," said Ginger.

"Yes," said William. "They'll surround the house an' set on us when we try to go out an'—an' no one'll ever know what's happened to us."

"The bomb might get 'em."

"It'll get us too if it does."

"Come on," said William. "I'm going to find a way out of this."

"Ole Bushy's gone back into his own house now."

"Oh, come *on*!" said William.

He had found a convenient drainpipe that ran down from a convenient gutter in close proximity to a convenient tree, and already he had swung one leg over the parapet, caught hold of a branch of the tree to steady himself and was making his way down the drainpipe. The others followed more slowly.

Reaching the ground, they stood and looked at each other.

"You've got cobwebs all over your face, William," said Ginger.

"So've you," said William. "So've all of us. We got 'em gettin' out of the window."

"What'll we do now?" said Henry.

"Let's go home," said Ginger. "The bomb'll be goin' off any minute."

"We can't go till we've saved Douglas from himself," said William. "That's what we set out to do an' we're goin' to *do* it. We've got to prove to him that ole Bushy's a crim'nal. We'll tell him about the bomb an' I bet that'll scare him off all right. . . . Come on. Let's see what he's doin' now."

They walked down the lane to the side gate of Roxborough, and, keeping in the shelter of the hedge, peered over it.

Mrs. Willingham sat on a garden seat knitting. Patsy was on the swing and Douglas was pushing her.

There was an ecstatic but somewhat exhausted look on Douglas's face.

"Gosh!" said William, wrinkling up his features (still obscured by a few cobwebs) in disgust. "Pushin' a *girl* on a *swing*! Ole *Douglas*!"

Patsy jumped off the swing and ran across the lawn, followed by Douglas.

"Wonder what they're goin' to do now," said William, forgetting caution and craning his neck over the gate.

At this point Mr. Willingham emerged from the french windows. Hastily but too late, William withdrew his head.

"Hello, hello, hello!" boomed Mr. Willingham. "An unexpected guest! *Three* unexpected guests! Come in, boys! Come in! Come in! Come in!"

Reluctantly they opened the gate and entered. Mr. Willingham sat down beside his wife on the garden seat, making an expansive gesture in the direction of the boys.

"Sit down! Sit down!" he said. "Make yourselves at home. I have a tale to unfold and I like as large an audience as possible."

William, Ginger and Henry sat down on the grass in front of the garden seat, Douglas and Patsy a little way distant from them. Douglas looked sheepish and avoided William's eye. Mr. Willingham turned to his wife.

"I have accepted the post," he said.

She raised her placid gaze from her knitting.

"Have you, dear?" she said.

"Are you glad?" he said.

"*Gosh!*" *said William* . . . "*pushin'* a girl *on a* swing! *Ole* Douglas!"

"I think it'll be nice, dear," she said. "A change is always a change."

"How true! How true!" said her husband. He turned again to the children. "But I must enlighten my audience. I must bring you into the picture. Perhaps you know that I edit a small paper called *Hobbies*. It deals, I need hardly add, with hobbies. . . . Well, I have had an offer to edit a similar paper, with perhaps, better prospects, in Scotland. For days my mind has been in a turmoil."

"Tossed on the horns of a dilemma," said Henry.

"Exactly, exactly," said Mr. Willingham. "Torn between two alternatives—to cling to the familiar, the secure, the humdrum, or launch out into the unknown, adventure into fresh woods and pastures new. To accept or reject the offer of work that might prove more interesting and profitable, but that would expose one to the icy winds of change, would involve one in new friendships, new contacts, a new background, new ideas, new outlook . . ."

"New carpets, new curtains . . ." murmured his wife.

"Exactly, exactly, my dear. You have put the whole thing in a nutshell. Well, as I said, my mind refused to come to a decision . . ."

"Last night, you know, dear," said his wife, "you said that you'd make up your mind today before sunset."

"I did, my dear, and I am a man of my word. I sat at my desk, dithering, hesitating, tossed to and fro on the waves of pros and cons, when suddenly I noticed that the sun was veering to the west and I remembered what I had said. The die must be cast before sunset. And suddenly I decided to leave the whole decision to the Goddess of Chance. I decided to take twenty-four steps down the lane with my eyes closed. Then I would open my eyes and if my surroundings were unchanged in every detail I would refuse the job, but if any change, however slight, had taken place in my surroundings while I was making my twenty-four steps with my eyes closed, then I would accept the job." He gave an apologetic chuckle. "It sounds too idiotic for words, doesn't it? I don't suppose you boys ever do anything as idiotic as that."

"We count cows," said William with dignity.

"Not a bad idea," said Mr. Willingham. "I'll try that next time."

"What happened?" said Henry.

"Well, I had a good look around me and noticed every detail. Then I closed my eyes and took my twenty-four steps. Then I stopped, opened my eyes, and looked around me again."

"And was there anything different?" said Patsy.

"Indeed there was, my child. There were people on the roof of Elm Mead who had not been there when I closed my eyes. I hadn't got my distance glasses with me and the trees are rather thick just there, but certainly there were people on the roof who had not been there before. I remembered that the agent had said that several tiles on the roof needed renewing and I supposed he'd sent someone along from the builders to look into it. . . . Anyway, I came home, rang up the people in Scotland and accepted the job. They want me at once so we shan't be here much longer. They've got a house lined up for us, so we can clear out of here any moment and leave this in the agent's hands. What do you think of that, my dear?"

"I've never been to Scotland," said Mrs. Willingham with her placid smile, "but I've always heard that it's very nice."

"As to you, my child," said Mr. Willingham to Patsy, "you vanish from the scenes tomorrow. I rang up your grandmother to ask if we might park you with her till we'd completed the move. Strange to say, she was delighted and is fetching you tomorrow."

"Oh, goody!" said Patsy.

Douglas gave her an anguished glance.

William, Henry and Ginger were gradually recovering from their stupefaction.

"About the bomb . . ." said William.

"What bomb?" said Mr. Willingham.

"The bomb in the garage . . . the garage of Elm Mead."

"Oh, that's not a bomb," said Mr. Willingham easily. "It's a box of indoor fireworks. Someone wanted to put an advertisement in *Hobbies* for indoor fireworks. They sounded a bit dangerous so I thought I'd try them out myself before I accepted the advert, and I asked for a box of them and brought it home from the office and slipped it into the garage of Elm Mead, so that this young woman wouldn't get hold of it and blow herself up. She's a nosey little creature, you know."

"Let's try them out now, Daddy," said Patsy.

"Well, I don't see why we shouldn't The sub-editor rang me up as soon as I'd got home and said that he'd tried them out and they were as harmless as mice. . . . Yes, let's celebrate by a fireworks display. Come on! I'll get them from the garage."

"They—they aren't in the garage," said William.

"Where are they?"

"Beside the tank in the loft," said William.

"Good Lord! How on earth did they get there?"

"We took them," said William simply.

"Oh well, I suppose you had your reasons," said Mr. Willingham. Evidently he was not a man to waste his time probing deeply into mysteries. "I'll nip along and get them."

He set off quickly towards the gate.

The boys stared at each other, stunned again into silence.

The four were walking slowly homewards. William and Ginger walked in front. Henry and Douglas followed. The indoor fireworks display had been a tremendous success. Glittering volcanos, fiery cascades, shooting stars and golden rain had lit up the darkened room, while sparklers and magic ferns filled any dull moment.

"It was smashin', wasn't it?" said Ginger.

"Yes, it jolly well was," said William. He turned back to look at Douglas. "An' we saved him from himself."

"Yes," agreed Ginger. "It took a bit of doin' but we did it all right."

They stood and waited for Henry and Douglas to join them, then all four walked on together. William threw a glance of affectionate solicitude at Douglas.

"What do you feel like now, Douglas?" he said. "Is it any better?"

"It's a bit better," said Douglas, "but it's awful to think I'll never see her again."

"You'll get over it, Douglas," said Henry.

"Yes, I s'pose I shall," said Douglas.

"You'd have got jolly bored in time," said Ginger. "Pushin' her on tricycles an' swingin' her on swings."

"Yes, I s'pose I should," said Douglas.

"You missed a smashin' time on Wednesday," said William. We climbed down to the pool at the bottom of the quarry an' sailed rafts on it. We could go an' do it again tomorrow. Would you like to?"

"Yes, I would," said Douglas. A note of eagerness had crept into his voice. "Yes, let's."

"You're really rather glad it's over, aren't you, Douglas?" said Henry.

"Well, it was a bit of a tie," admitted Douglas, "but"— he sighed deeply—"it was a great experience."

CHAPTER V

WILLIAM AND THE ART CLUB

No one could ever remember who first had the idea of the Art Club. The village had had clubs innumerable— Literary Clubs, Dramatic Clubs, Debating Clubs, Brass-Rubbing Clubs, Gardening Clubs, Flower Arranging Clubs—not to speak of the inevitable Cricket, Tennis, Bowls and Rugger Clubs—but it had never before had an Art Club.

Miss Golightly, as the headmistress of Rose Mount School and the upholder of Culture in all its local branches, was naturally the President, and most of the inhabitants of the village enrolled themselves as members, less from any deep interest in art than from a desire to be in anything that was going on.

The Outlaws took little interest in all this till they heard that the post of secretary had been offered to Archie Mannister, the only practising (if as yet unrecognised) artist in the neighbourhood and that Archie had declined the position. Archie was so vague and feckless and diffident and impractical that one only had to look at him to realise that he needed someone to protect and champion him. And the Outlaws had long ago constituted themselves his champions and protectors.

"Gosh! He's turned it down," said William, reporting

106

the affair to Ginger, Henry and Douglas in the old barn. "He's turned it *down*! Jus' the thing that might have made him important an' he's turned it down. People'd stop thinkin' he was a rotten artist if he was secret'ry of somethin'. Secret'ries are important people an' it's time Archie did somethin' to make him important. People might buy his pictures if he was secret'ry of somethin' an' he might even get his photo in the newspapers."

"It might even help him get into the Royal Academy or the British Museum," said Douglas.

"Not just at first," said Henry, "but it would be a step. It would help him keep his name before the public. My father knows a man that does advertising an' he says that it's very important these days to keep one's name before the public."

"Well, if he's turned it down we can't do anythin' about it," said Ginger.

"I don't think he's actually turned it down," said Henry. "My fam'ly were talkin' about it this mornin'. He tried to turn it down 'cause jus' the thought of it scared him to death—but they made him promise to think it over."

"Come on, then," said William. There was a note of resolution in his voice. "Let's go'n' help him think it over."

"We'll put it to him," said Henry.

"Yes," said William, "we'll put it to him."

They found Archie's studio in its usual state of chaos, with Archie busily at work on a piece of still life. The still life had originally consisted of a daffodil in a jar placed next to a piece of Stilton cheese on a plate. Archie had begun it yesterday, but he had forgotten to put any water in the jar and he had absent-mindedly eaten the cheese, so that he was working now chiefly from memory.

"I can't quite remember the colour of the cheese," he

said. "I know it had a tinge of yellow, but, of course, it should be a different shade of yellow from the daffodil."

"We've come to talk to you, Archie," said William earnestly.

"To put it to you," said Ginger.

"To keep your name before the public," said Henry.

"To get you hung in the British Museum," said Douglas.

"What *are* you talking about?" said Archie testily, but his still life was getting on his nerves and he was rather glad of the interruption.

"It's about you bein' secret'ry of the Art Club," said William.

A look of panic came into Archie's thin face.

"Oh, I couldn't . . ." he said. "I couldn't possibly. I just couldn't take on a thing like that. I told them so."

"Why not?" said William. "You're an artist."

"Yes, but art . . . I mean art in general . . . I—I just don't know enough about it."

"We'll help you," said Henry.

"We know something about art," said William.

"We learn it at school," said Douglas. "We have *lessons* in it."

"I drew a picture of a volcano last week," said Ginger, "an' my mother said it was abs'lutely realistic."

"She thought it was meant to be a pineapple," said William.

"Oh, shut up," said Ginger.

"This is all just rubbish," said Archie sternly.

"But listen, Archie," said Henry. "Havin' a position like that—secret'ry of an Art Club—it'd be good for you professionally."

"It might bring you a lot more customers," said William.

"Clients," said Ginger.

"Sitters," said Henry.

"Well, whatever it is it'd bring you more of 'em," said William.

"Y—yes," said Archie, "but the fact remains that

"We've come to talk to you Archie," said William earnestly.

I'm not businesslike and that a secretary ought to be businesslike."

"We'd see to that part of it for you," said William airily. "We're *jolly* businesslike. You needn't worry about that."

"My mother always gets our meat at Hoskins' 'cause he rings the bell in church," said Ginger, "so that shows that bein' important makes a diff'rence to a person's career."

"But I keep telling you," protested Archie. "I—I couldn't possibly—I'd make a mess of the whole thing. I'm always losing letters and forgetting things."

"We'll help you look for the things you've lost," said William. "We like lookin' for things."

"And we'll remind you of the things you've forgotten," said Ginger.

"You'll regret it all your life if you don't," said Henry solemnly.

Archie was obviously thinking deeply. . . . He seemed to come to a sudden decision. His thin anxious face tensed resolutely. He strode to his desk, removed from it a half-eaten sandwich, a clothes-brush, a dishcloth, a pullover, and a box of paints, dumped them on the hearthrug, dug out a writing-pad from beneath a laundry bag and, finding a biro after much searching in the date-box where he kept his mending materials, sat down at his desk and began to write. Then, taking an envelope that marked a place in his telephone directory, he addressed it and handed it to William.

"Drop that in Miss Golightly's letterbox," he said. "For better or worse, I've accepted the secretaryship."

"The die is cast," said Henry.

The first meeting of the Committee of the Art Club took place the next week.

The Outlaws stood at the gate of Archie's cottage, awaiting his return.

"He's a long time comin'," said William anxiously.

"I bet he's got into a muddle," said Douglas.

"I hope he's not got the sack already," said Ginger.

"Here he is!" said William.

Archie's figure could be seen at the bend of the road.

He walked slowly and carefully, his chin resting on a pile of books that he carried in his arms, dropping a few at intervals during his progress. The Outlaws ran to meet him. They picked up the books and accompanied him into the cottage.

"You've been a long time, Archie," said William.

"Yes," said Archie, letting the pile of books slide to the floor. "I went to the Hadley Library to get some art books. I thought I'd better brush up my general background. It's a bit vague."

"But what about the meeting?" said William impatiently.

"You've not got the sack yet, have you, Archie?" said Douglas.

"Oh, no . . . Not yet . . ." said Archie reassuringly. "They were all very kind. Miss Golightly said that she was sure that with time and patience we'd get on fairly well." He picked up a book and began to turn the pages. "Early Etruscan art . . . Perhaps I needn't have got this out . . . I don't suppose we shall touch on it . . ."

"But what are you goin' to *do* in this club?" said William.

"Oh, yes," said Archie, closing the book. "There was a lot of discussion as to what the activities should consist of. Miss Thompson suggested Folk Dancing classes and General Moult wanted to hold an exhibition of his South African curios. It would have been a good idea, of course, but everyone's seen them so often. Mrs. Bott wanted to show her coloured photographs of the Isle of Wight and she resigned from the committee when they voted against it, so finally it was decided that the first activity should be an outing to inspect the art treasures of some stately home in the neighbourhood."

"My aunt's got a sort of art treasure," said Douglas.

"It's a sort of statue of a gnome in the garden, painted red."

"Oh, no, no!" said Archie. "That's not the sort of thing at all. I mean pictures by old masters and things like that."

"Where are there any?" said Henry.

"That's what I have to find out," said Archie. "My first duty as a secretary is to find out. I must set the wheels in motion."

Archie set the wheels in motion, at first with little success. Sir Gerald and Lady Markham explained apologetically that their ancestors had been of a sporting rather than artistic nature and had collected trophies of the chase (the Manor fairly bristled with antlers) rather than artistic masterpieces. Sir Gervase Torrance of Steedham said that he had inherited a Romney, a Fragonard and a couple of Girtins from his father, but had sold them to help pay for the upkeep of his private zoo.

"After all, what's the point of the things?" he said. "Just bits of paint dabbed on to pieces of canvas. . . . I'd rather have a live giraffe any day."

Archie had almost given up hope when he heard quite by chance that Applelea Court contained a reputed Gainsborough, a doubtful Stubbs and a painting of a country scene "believed to be by Constable". It wasn't spectacular but it was better than nothing.

The Outlaws, paying him their usual routine visit to see how he was progressing in his new duties and offer their assistance, found him looking harassed and distraught, just replacing the telephone receiver.

"Oh dear!" he said. "Yes, she's got them. . . . Mrs. Herriot of Applelea Court. . . . The reputed Gainsborough and Stubbs and Constable, but it seems she breeds dogs . . . poodles, I mean."

"Well, that makes it all the more int'resting," said William. "Dogs'll be a nice change from pictures."

"No, it complicates the whole situation " said Archie. "She says she's completely booked up with shows and things except for tomorrow. She wants us to go tomorrow. It's all such a rush. I feel I'm being driven from pillar to post. . . . I've been in touch with the members and they can all manage it, but it means I must go over there this afternoon to see the pictures before I make my notes for the talk. I'm beginning to wish I'd never taken it on. I don't even know where the place is."

"We'll take you there," said William.

"We know the way," said Ginger.

"There's safety in numbers," said Henry.

"We'll help you with the pillars and posts," said Douglas.

Archie considered the suggestion. He would be going into the unknown and he always shrank from the unknown. For the moment the Outlaws seemed to be tried and trusted friends. Almost before he knew what he was doing he had accepted their company.

"All right," he said, adding hastily, "as long as you don't do anything outrageous."

"I dunno what you mean, Archie," said William coldly. "We're comin' to *help* you."

"Very well," said Archie weakly, "but I wish I knew where it was all going to end."

Mrs. Herriot of Applelea Court was a little surprised to see her guest enter the drawing-room followed by the four boys.

"Dear me!" she said. "I suggested that you brought an art expert or art experts with you, but surely these aren't——"

"No, no," Archie assured her nervously. "They aren't art experts. Not really. I mean, n-not exactly. . . ."

"We came to show him the way here," said William, giving her his glassy smile.

"And back," said Ginger.

"I see," said Mrs. Herriot.

She was a large thick-set woman with a dominating presence and a deep voice. Her hair was "Eton cropped" and she wore tweeds of a somewhat violent shade. As she rose from her seat to greet them she seemed to be advancing on them in battle formation.

"Well, let's waste no time," she said. "We'll go and see the pictures at once."

As she spoke a little girl emerged from behind the curtains. She was about seven years old, with a freckled face and carroty hair done up in pigtails. A stick of rock protruded from her mouth and she dangled a shapeless rag doll by its top-knot.

"This is my little god-daughter," said Mrs. Herriot. "She's here on a short visit while her parents go fishing. Say 'how d'you do', darling."

The child removed the stick of rock from her mouth, gave each of the Outlaws a long cold stare then replaced the rock.

"Show them your dolly, darling," said Mrs. Herriot. "Tell them her name."

The child continued to suck the rock in silence.

"She's shy," explained Mrs. Herriot. "Sweet but shy. She's called Andalusia—the child, I mean—after the place where her parents spent their honeymoon, and the doll's called Boadicea after Britain's warrior queen. Now come along. Let's find the paintings."

They formed a little procession. Andalusia took her place next to William.

"What's your name?" she said, detaching herself again from her stick of rock.

William ignored her.

"You can have a lick of my rock if you like."

William continued to ignore her.

"I've got a fur muff."

William still ignored her.

"Real fur. Mink."

William remained silent.

"I've been to the South of France in an aeroplane. I—I got a *prize* for dancing." Her voice rose shrilly in exasperation. "*Say* something."

William's whole attention seemed to be given to the ceiling. She jabbed him in the ribs with her stick of rock and contorted her features into a grimace of anger and contempt. William turned and did his Face at her.

For a moment she was startled into silence, then raised her voice in a shrill scream. Mrs. Herriot looked back at her and shrugged resignedly.

"Temperamental," she said. "Sweet but temperamental."

William took advantage of the diversion to hurry forward and join Ginger, and the procession continued on its way to the dining-room.

The dining-room was large and magnificently furnished. The reputed Gainsborough hung over the chimney piece— a painting of a dreamy-looking female in diaphanous robes, wearing a large feathered hat, seated on a bank in a rustic setting, with a dog of indeterminate breed lying at her feet.

"This," said Mrs. Herriot, "is the reputed Gainsborough. Personally I'm convinced that it's a genuine Gainsborough. Only such a master artist as Gainsborough could have painted it. It has the Gainsborough *touch*. It's not unlike the portrait of Mrs. Robinson in the Wallace Collection, though, of course, it has its points of difference. . . . Now, Mr. Mannister, would you, as an art expert, consider this a genuine Gainsborough?"

Archie looked wildly at the picture and gibbered unin-

"There's very little doubt about this," said Mrs. Herriot.

telliglby for a few moments. Then he cleared his throat with a startlingly explosive sound.

"It m-might be," said. "On the other hand it m-might not."

"Exactly," said Mrs. Herriot. "That seems to be the

general opinion. Personally I incline to the view that it *is* a genuine Gainsborough. That black velvet ribbon round the neck . . . *so* typical. Well, let's go on to the Stubbs. The Stubbs is in the library."

She led the way into a spacious book-lined room with a marble bust of Cicero on the chimney-piece and, above it, the painting of a large brown cart-horse, standing in a large green field, nibbling a hedge.

"Well, what is your opinion of that, Mr. Mannister? *Is* it a Stubbs?"

Archie blinked distractedly at the picture then cleared his throat again.

"Well, it m-might be," he said. "It might qu-quite well be. On the other hand, it might just as w-well not be."

"But surely only Stubbs could have painted such a— well, such a *horselike* horse. After all, he was the *king* of horse painters. Personally I have no doubt at all that it's a genuine Stubbs. Now come and see the Constable."

The Constable hung in the hall. It represented a rather vague country scene, containing a dilapidated cottage and a farm-cart.

"There's very little doubt about this," said Mrs. Herriot. "It has the Constable *touch*. . . . Notice the farm-cart. There's nearly always a farm-cart—or something like it—in Constable's paintings. What do you think, Mr. Mannister?"

Archie's mouth moved silently as he searched in vain for words. Mrs. Herriot made an imperious gesture.

"Well, you'll bring your club along tomorrow and give your talk, won't you? I shall look forward to it. . . . And now you must come and see the dogs."

She led them out of the house and down to the old stables. The Outlaws walked in silence, overawed by their surroundings. Andalusia brought up the rear, sucking her stick of rock, dangling Boadicea by the top-knot and glaring at the back of William's head.

Outside the stables, a large enclosure contained poodles of every size and shade. They ran barking to the wire netting as the visitors approached.

"Adorable, aren't they?" said Mrs. Herriot, "And brimming with intelligence . . . but come and see the ones in the stables."

Inside the stables were rows of wired-in boxes. Maternal poodle faces gazed anxiously through the wires and small dark figures sprawled over each other at their feet. Mrs. Herriot opened one of the boxes and took out a black curly-haired puppy.

"This is Topsy," she said. "He's perfect, isn't he? Perfect teeth, thin tail, short back, small feet lovely leathers. And look at his eyes. Perfect ovals. And sturdy, too. Quite ready to leave his mother. Just over ten weeks old." She turned suddenly to Archie and held out the puppy. "I'd like you to have him, Mr. Mannister."

"Oh, no, *no*!" said Archie, backing away apprehensively.

"Yes, you must," said Mrs. Herriot, thrusting the puppy into his arms. "You *must* have him. I want you to. I know you'll give him a good home. You'll find him a wonderful little companion and they make splendid house dogs."

"Oh, but I c-couldn't," stammered Archie. "I c-c-c-c-couldn't."

"Yes, I insist," said Mrs. Herriot. "In a week's time you won't know how you managed to live without him."

"Oh, but p-p-please," said Archie. "It's so very kind of you, b-but——"

"Don't thank me, my dear man. It's a pleasure."

The Outlaws crowded round Archie and the puppy.

"Let me hold him, Archie."

"Gosh! He's *super*, Archie!"

"He wants to come with you, Archie. Look at him wagging his tail."

"Well, I'm afraid you must go now," said Mrs. Herriot, briskly. "I have a lot of things to see to indoors. Good-bye, Mr. Mannister. Good-bye, boys. I shall expect you with the club to-morrow, Mr. Mannister. I'm looking forward to your talk. Good-bye!"

Dazed and bewildered, clutching the puppy to his chest, Archie set off down the drive.

At the bend of the drive a sound between a howl and a scream made them turn round. Mrs. Herriot stood calmly watching them but Andalusia had hurled her stick of rock on to the ground and was battering Mrs. Herriot about the knees with Boadicea in what appeared to be an access of rage.

They turned into the road and the boys scuffled for possession of the puppy.

"I bet he'll soon learn to do tricks."

"He's tryin' to play with me."

"He's jolly strong. He's got a sort of bloodhound grip."

"Oh dear!" moaned Archie as he surrendered the puppy to them. "A dog on top of everything else! I don't know . . . I can't think . . . I don't even know what I'm going to feed it on. I've got nothing in the house but a soused herring."

"Don't worry about that, Archie," said William. "We'll bring you lots of things for it to eat."

"I'll take it back tomorrow after the talk," said Archie. "I can't give my mind to anything till that's over."

"We'll stay an' help you with it till bedtime," said William. "We've got to go to school tomorrow mornin' but it's the half holiday so we'll come along first thing in the afternoon."

They went along first thing in the afternoon. They had stayed till bedtime the day before, playing with the puppy and offering it various titbits that they fetched from their homes. It had refused Ginger's sardine, William's pineapple chunks and Douglas's toffee apple, but Henry had profited by his parents' absence to abstract a fairly large portion of chicken from the fridge. He had cut it into small pieces with his penknife and the puppy had eaten it with every appearance of enjoyment. They had departed reluctantly at bedtime, leaving Archie sitting at his desk surrounded by art books, with the puppy happily engaged in chewing up the hearthrug.

"It doesn't seem to be anywhere about," said William,

looking anxiously round the empty garden. "I thought it'd be guardin' the house."

"They have to be specially trained for that," said Henry.

"They have to learn the diff'rence between crim'nals an' non-crim'nals," said Ginger.

"I think crim'nals have a special smell," said Douglas.

The entered the cottage and pushed open the door of the studio.

Archie sat at his desk in an attitude of despair, gazing at a piece of paper that lay in front of him. He turned a haggard face to them as they entered.

"She's sent a bill," he said.

"A what?" said William.

"A bill. A bill for thirty guineas."

"What for?" said William.

"The dog," groaned Archie. "The dog! I thought she was giving it me."

"Well, wasn't she?"

"No. She's sent me a bill. Thirty guineas. I haven't *got* thirty guineas."

"It might be a mistake," said Henry. "It might be meant for someone else with the same name as yours. Why don't you ring her up about it?"

"I have done," said Archie, "and there isn't any mistake. She says I must pay the thirty guineas or take the dog back."

"Well, take the dog back."

Archie flung out his arms wildly.

"I can't. It's gone."

"Gone!" gasped William. "It was here last night."

"I know. It was here when I went to bed. I put it on a cushion on the kitchen chair and this morning—well, it just wasn't there."

"Have you looked for it?"

121

"Looked for it! I've ransacked every nook and cranny. I've looked everywhere—even in the cupboards and drawers. I've even looked in the saucepans. She was most unpleasant about it. She said if I couldn't produce either the money or the dog she'd put the matter in the hands of her solicitors." His features twisted in anguish. "I shall be ruined. Literally ruined . . . And I'm supposed to be giving the art talk this afternoon. How can I concentrate on art with my future wrecked, my name dishonoured, and this sword of whoever it was hanging over my head?"

"Damocles" said Henry.

"We'll find it for you, Archie," said William soothingly. "We'll go an' look for it now an' I bet we'll have found it in ten minutes."

But a thorough search of cottage, garden and surrounding countryside revealed no trace of the missing poodle. They returned to the cottage, where Archie sat gazing mournfully over his mountain of art books.

"It'll mean the end of my career," he said. "It's the sort of thing people never forget. They'll hold it against me to my dying day. Dog thief, she called me! I shall have to appear in court and probably go to prison. I shall be branded as a criminal for the rest of my life."

"No, you won't, Archie," said William "We'll get that dog back for you somehow."

"An' they often let first offenders off," said Henry. " 'Specially if they've got a good character."

"An' you've got a good character, Archie," said Douglas. "You've done brass-rubbings in church."

Archie glanced at his watch and uttered another groan.

"Oh, Jehosophat! It's time I started for the talk. I shall have to go through with it. It's too late to get out of it. Oh, dear! I shall never keep my ideas clear with disgrace

and imprisonment staring me in the face. A *dog* thief! . . .
Where are my notes?"

He began to burrow among the chaotic mass of papers
that covered his desk.

William had drawn the other three out into the garden.

"I've got an idea," he whispered.

"What?" said Ginger.

"She's sent a bill," said Archie.

"It'll have to be a jolly quick idea," said Henry. "Time's
running short."

"It won't be any good whatever it is," said Douglas.
"He's doomed."

"Oh, shut up," said William. "It's a jolly good idea, an'
it's a quick one, too. We've got to help him pay that
thirty guineas."

"How can we?" said Ginger. "We haven't any money."

123

"I spent my last ha'penny on that toffee apple," said Douglas gloomily, "an' it wouldn't touch it."

"I know we haven't any money," said William, "but we've got to find valu'ble things to give her in part payment an' then we'll save up money to pay the other part later."

"Well, what have we got that's valu'ble?" said Ginger.

"There's Roderick," said William. "He's s'posed to be, isn't he?"

"Y-yes," said Ginger. Roderick was a black and white rabbit that his uncle had given him on his last birthday. Ginger had not yet quite come to terms with him. "Y-yes . . . he's a good *sort* of rabbit. He's been to rabbit shows."

"I bet he's as valu'ble as that ole puppy anyway," said William, "an' you wouldn't miss him much. You said you thought he despised you."

"Well, he does seem to," said Ginger. "He's got that sort of look on his face when he looks at me."

"I think it's jus' the way his mouth is made," said Douglas. "I think he's tryin' to smile."

"Oh, stop wastin' *time*," said William tersely. "Now, come on. What else can we take in part payment? What else can we take in part payment? What about your mouse, Henry?"

Henry's father had given him a new camera as a reward for keeping the lawn mown and the garden tidy while he (Henry's father) was incapacitated by a badly sprained ankle. Henry had swopped his old camera (which was in an advanced state of decrepitude) for Victor Jameson's mouse. It was a plump brownish mouse that spent most of its time in its sleeping quarters, emerging occasionally to eat or trot round its little wheel in a determined if rather dreamy fashion.

"You've only had it for a week," went on William. "You can't have got fond of it."

"I'm *beginnin'* to get fond of it," said Henry with a note of regret in his voice.

"Not very valu'ble, a mouse," said Douglas.

"I bet *this* one is," said Henry, rising hotly to the defence of his mouse. "It's got some white hairs on its chest an' I've never seen another mouse with white hairs on its chest jus' like that. It—it's a phenonemon. It's probably beyond price."

"Not much use to us, then," said Douglas. "What else have we got?"

"I'll take my motor horn," said William. "The one with the rubber squeezer. I'd thought of keepin' it till I die an' leavin' it to the British Museum in my will."

"You bought it at a jumble sale for sixpence," said Ginger.

"Yes, but they didn't realise its *value*," said William. "They didn't realise that it was a valu'ble piece of antiquity. You only see them in *very* veteran cars an' they'll get rarer an' rarer as time goes on till mine's the only one left in the whole world. I bet it's more valu'ble than any ole black dog. What'll you bring, Douglas?"

"I could bring my conker," said Douglas after a slight hesitation.

Douglas had an ancient conker of colossal proportions that he cherished devotedly, polishing it at intervals and keeping it locked up in an old brief-case of his father's.

"I don't see that that'll be much good," said Ginger.

" 'Course it will," said Douglas. "There isn't another like it in the whole world. It's a—a phenomenon, same as the hooter an' Henry's mouse. It'd make a jolly good weapon, too. It's strong as iron. It'd *brain* anyone if it hit them on the right spot."

"Well, that makes four. Let's go 'n' fetch 'em as quick as we can. We must get her alone first an' 'splain to her an' do a bit of pleadin' for Archie before we give her the part-payment an' we mus' get it all fixed up before Archie starts his talk. He'll be too worried to talk about art with that dog on his mind."

They ran home and met a short time later at the corner of the road that led to William's house. William inspected their contributions with satisfaction.

"It's a super part-payment," he said.

"Shouldn't be surprised if it turns out to be a full payment," said Ginger. "It's valu'ble all right."

"But we'll have to be jolly careful," said William. "We mustn't let her see them till we can get her alone an' do the pleadin' with her."

"How can we stop her seein' them?" said Henry.

"We can keep 'em hidden. You can keep your mouse in your pocket an' Douglas can keep his conker in his pocket an' I'll keep my hooter under my pullover an' Ginger can keep Roderick under his."

They concealed the part-payments as best they could and set off down the road.

But Roderick was proving difficult. He refused to be accommodated under Ginger's pullover. He squirmed and wriggled and pushed and pulled and tried to edge his way out.

"Let's swop," said William. "You take the hooter an' I'll take Roderick. I'm jolly good at carryin' things under my pullover. I've carried heavier things than rabbits. I once carried a radio 'cause I wanted to pretend to be a pop singer."

"Yes, an' you turned on the wrong station an' came out with bagpipes," said Ginger.

"Well, it's jolly difficult turnin' on a station under a

126

pullover," said William. "Anyway, let's start off. An' we'd better be quick. She might be gettin' him arrested any minute now."

He pushed Roderick under his pullover. Roderick seemed to settle down fairly comfortably in his new quarters and they set off in the direction of Applelea Court.

Archie had evidently set off before them. They saw him entering the gates of the Court, his arms piled with books and note-books. A few slithered to the ground as he turned into the gateway and he did not stop to retrieve them. The Outlaws gathered them up as best they could and followed him to the front door, where he was already in conversation with Mrs. Herriot. Mrs. Herriot looked at them coldly.

"What are these boys doing here?" she said.

"We're carryin' Mr. Mannister's books for him," said William, assuming an air of hauteur and hitching Roderick into a more comfortable position.

Archie threw them a startled glance then turned again to Mrs. Herriot.

"But I thought you were *giving* it to me," he wailed.

"My good man, I *was* giving it to you," said Hrs. Herriot. "Thirty guineas for a *perfect* little specimen like that. I was simply *giving* it away. But I must, of course, insist on the thirty guineas."

"But I haven't got it," moaned Archie.

"Then return the dog."

"I haven't got that either," said Archie. "It's gone."

"So you said on the telephone. I don't know who you're in league with, my good man—dog thieves or vivisectionists—but——"

Archie gave a squeal of protest.

"I'm n-not," he gibbered. "I swear I'm not. I—I—
I——"

"Well, as I told you, I shall put the matter in the hands of my solicitor."

"Listen," began William but Mrs. Herriot's eyes were fixed on the bend of the drive where already the members of the Art Club were appearing, led by Miss Golightly and General Moult.

"We'll postpone this discussion till later," she said. She held out her hand to Miss Golightly. "Welcome to Applelea Court! I shall be delighted to show you my little treasures."

The Art Club murmured its gratitude. Miss Golightly said that the frontage of the house suggested Tudor influence with Jacobean additions, and General Moult said it reminded him of some building in South Africa, but he couldn't quite remember which.

"We mus' get her alone," whispered William, "an' do the bit of *pleadin'* . . ."

"Before you see the actual paintings," Mrs. Herriot was saying, "I should like to show you the formal garden at the back of the house. It's a very fine example. There's a tradition that John Evelyn had a hand in the planning of it. You see it best from the landing window and I'm afraid that, to reach it, we must go through the room that's being used as my little goddaughter's bedroom while she's staying with me. She left orders (Mrs. Herriot smiled indulgently) that no one was to go into the room because her doll Boadicea was suffering from measles and mustn't be disturbed, but I think we might perhaps venture . . ."

Roderick was growing restive. Miss Thompson threw nervous glances at the strange upheavals that were taking place beneath William's pullover.

128

"Are you feeling quite well, dear boy?" she said anxiously.

William gave her a stony stare.

"Yes, thank you," he said.

They ascended the staircase.

Mrs. Herriot approached a white painted door and tried the handle. It didn't move. She tried it again. Still it didn't move.

"You can't come in," called Andalusia shrilly. "I've locked it. Boadicea's very ill. She mustn't be disturbed. She'll *die* if she's disturbed."

"Oh, darling," said Mrs. Herriot. "Don't be difficult. We won't disturb Boadicea. We only want to go through the room."

There was a short silence, then: "Will you promise to walk on tiptoe and not *look* at her. She's so ill that she'd *die* if anyone looked at her."

"Yes, dear."

"You'll tiptoe and you won't *look* at her?"

"Of course, darling," said Mrs. Herriot impatiently.

"You *promise*?"

"Yes, yes, yes."

The key was turned in the lock. The Art Club entered. It was a bright sunny room. A doll's cot stood by the window, its curtains closely drawn. Andalusia stood beside it, scowling darkly, her finger at her lips.

"Tiptoe," she said fiercely, "an' don't speak a *word* an' don't come *near* her."

Meekly the Art Club began to tiptoe in single file across the room towards the farther door. But Roderick was losing patience. The volcanic upheavals beneath William's pullover were becoming more violent each second . . . till suddenly he gave a plunge and, escaping William's restraining hand, descended with a plop on to the floor.

129

The Art Club stood, paralysed by amazement. But Roderick was far from paralysed. He ran across the floor towards the window, bumping against the doll's cot, which stood in his way . . . and suddenly all was confusion. For the doll's cot overturned, ejecting a small black creature, wearing a frilly bonnet and a short frilly white frock. Despite these encumbrances, it frisked in a light-hearted fashion round the room in pursuit of Roderick.

"Topsy!" screamed Mrs. Herriot.

She plunged towards him, colliding with Henry and sending him headlong to the ground. The mouse escaped from his pocket and joined in the race. Miss Milton, true to the training of her youth, screamed and leapt upon the nearest chair. William, intent on capturing the mouse, tripped over Henry and fell heavily upon the bulb of his motor horn, which emitted a loud and raucous moan, adding to the general tumult. Then Douglas lost his head and aimed his conker wildly at Mrs. Herriot, catching Miss Golightly neatly over one eye. Above the uproar rose the shrill voice of Andalusia.

"I wanted to keep him. I didn't want you to give him away. You're a nasty horrid woman to give him away. I *liked* him. I wanted to keep him, and I followed those horrid boys and that horrid man back to their horrid little house to see where they lived and I got up early this morning and went there and the door wasn't locked and I found Topsy and brought him back and I *disguised* him as Boadicea and he *liked* being here. He's been asleep nearly all morning. I was going to keep him for ever and ever and now——"

Her voice ended on a scream then stopped abruptly. She grew purple in the face, her eyes bulged, her breath came in short gasps.

"Oh! dear!" said Mrs. Herriot. "That's what she does
130

"Topsy!" screamed Mrs. Herriot.

131

when she gets upset. It's a sort of attack. It terrifies me. I'm always afraid that something will burst inside her."

They all clustered around Andalusia, petting, soothing, condoling.

"But what's happened?" said Miss Golightly, rubbing her eye.

"It's William Brown that's happened," said Miss Milton, descending from her chair. "When is it ever anything else?"

"But where *is* William Brown?" said Miss Thompson, turning to look round the room.

William had gone, and with him had gone Ginger, Henry and Douglas. Taking advantage of Andalusia's "attack", they had collected the hooter, the conker, the mouse and the rabbit and made their way quietly, almost soundlessly, from the room. They were now walking quickly along the lane that led homewards. Ginger swung the hooter with a martial air, Douglas examined his conker anxiously for dents and polished it on the sleeve of his blazer. The mouse reposed peacefully in Henry's pocket. Roderick, stimulated by his recent adventure, surged and eddied beneath William's pullover.

"I still think they'd have been a super part-payment," said William, "but I'm glad we didn't have to pay them. I'd have missed my motor horn."

"And me my conker," said Douglas.

"And me my mouse," said Henry.

"And me Roderick," said Ginger.

They had reached a gap in the hedge through which they could see the chimneys and turrets of Applelea Court. They stopped for a moment to look at them

"I expect Archie's well away with his art talk now," said William.

William was right.

Peace had been restored at Applelea Court. Andalusia had been promised that Topsy should be her property during her visit to her godmother. Having gained her point, she had promptly lost interest in him and was nursing Boadicea through successive attacks of measles, scarlet fever, mumps, toothache and bronchitis, while Topsy had returned to his favourite occupation of chewing the hearthrug.

And Archie was well away with his art talk.

Light-hearted and light-headed with relief, he did not notice that his notes were in wild disorder, did not notice that he was in the library and not in the dining-room, did not even notice that the picture before him was not the reputed Gainsborough but the doubtful Stubbs.

His voice rose, high and fluty, as he read aloud from the notes he held in his hand.

"This must be one of the finest examples of our artist's work. Notice the delicate features, the bewitching turn of the neck, the hint of a smile in the curves of the lips, the humorous but intelligent expression of the eyes, the indescribable grace of the subject's posture . . ."

With growing bewilderment, but a dogged determination to master the subtleties of art, the members of the Art Club fixed their earnest gaze on the picture of the cart-horse nibbling the hedge. . . .

CHAPTER VI

THE PLAY'S THE THING

"WHY," said William, flinging out his arms in an expansive gesture, "does everyone in the whole world have a good time but me?"

Mrs. Brown looked at him apprehensively. He was evidently working himself up into one of his bouts of eloquence. She found them wearing.

"I don't know what you're talking about, dear," she said.

"You an' Dad an' Robert an' Ethel goin' out to dinner-parties an' theatres an'—an' theatres an' dinner-parties an' me jus' left at home same as that girl in the Sleepin' Beauty fairy tale an'——"

"You're thinking of Cinderella, dear," said Mrs. Brown.

"Well, whoever it was. Jus' left at home to *starve* for all you care," said William, his eloquence gathering force. "Gosh! There's *laws* against people goin' out an' leavin' their children at home to starve. Well, it's news to *me* if there's not laws to stop people goin' out an' leavin' their children at home to starve."

"I don't see how you can starve on the food I've got for you, William," said Mrs. Brown mildly.

"Food!" said William, dismissing food with another expansive gesture. "*Anythin'* might happen to me left alone at home like that an' you'd regret it for the rest of your life."

"You won't be alone, dear," said Mrs. Brown. "You'll

have Ginger and Henry and Douglas, and I've got some nice new constructional kits for you."

"Yes, while you're all out enjoyin' yourselves at dinner-parties an' theatres an'—an' livin' lives of lux'ry an' pleasure. Children that get neglected by their parents goin' out to lead lives of lux'ry an' pleasure turn into crim'nals when they grow up—I've read about it in newspapers—so you can't blame me if I turn into one after this. It'll be your fault if I start doin' smash an' grab raids an' stealin' money out of gas meters an' forgin' bank notes when I grow up. It'll be all your fault for neglectin' me an' leavin' me at home while you all go out enjoyin' yourselves. An' there's another thing——"

"Now, William——" began Mrs. Brown, but it was impossible to check William in midstream.

"People are goin' to think it's jolly *funny*. Well, I'm your son same as Robert, aren't I? Well, people'll think it jolly *funny*, you takin' one son out to dinner-parties an' things an' leavin' the other at home. They'll think you're *ashamed* of me. They'll think there's somethin' *wrong* with me. They——"

He paused for breath and Mrs. Brown seized her opportunity.

"Now listen, William. I've explained the situation to you over and over again. It's the opening night of the Hadley New Theatre and naturally your father got tickets for us, but he never thought of getting one for you. It's a new play that's going to be put on in London next month and it didn't sound a suitable play for children——"

"Children!" put in William with a bitter laugh. "I'm eleven, aren't I? Well, it's news to *me* that a person of eleven's a *child*."

"William, do stop using that idiotic expression," said Mrs. Brown wearily, "and just listen to me for a few
135

minutes. Your father got the four tickets for himself and me and Robert and Ethel and thought it would be nice for us all to meet and have dinner at the Grand Hotel in Hadley first, so he booked a table and we're all meeting there and—well, that's how things are. I know that it turned out that the play was just an ordinary thriller and we did try to get an extra seat for you when we discovered that, but the whole house was booked up so we couldn't. Actually it was booked up for all the week."

"An' Hubert Lane's goin'," said William, a note of desperation creeping into his voice. "Goin' in a box! It'll be jolly nice for me, won't it, Hubert Lane crowin' over me in a box!"

Mrs. Brown sighed. That, she knew, was the heart of the grievance. William had been content with the informal party of Ginger, Henry and Douglas in his home till he heard that the parents of Hubert Lane, his arch foe, had taken a box for the performance and that Hubert was to accompany them. Hubert was, of course, exploiting the situation to the best of his ability, jeering at the Outlaws, becoming daily bolder in his new-found assurance.

"Yah!" he jeered. "Peter Pan's more your line, isn't it! Yah! Kids!"

"Aunt Hester's coming to be with you, you know," said Mrs. Brown, "and she'll probably bring you some little present."

"Yes, an' *that's* jolly nice for us' isn't it?" said William with increasing bitterness, "havin' a *baby sitter* at home while you all go out eatin' things off menus an' watchin' plays!"

"Now listen, William——" began Mrs Brown again, but William had embarked on another stream of eloquence and was well away.

"An' it's a play about a murder an' who did it, isn't it? Well, if anyone ought to see that play, it's me. I've *written* plays about murders an' who did 'em. *The Bloody Hand* was about a murder an' who did it an' it was a jolly good play. Ginger said it was the best play he'd ever seen in his life an' he ought to know. He once learnt a whole speech out of Shakespeare to get two an' six out of his aunt, so he ought to know about *plays*. An' gosh!—Hubert Lane seein' it! In a *box*!"

Again Mrs. Brown sighed. She had planned for him an evening that she thought would amply compensate for missing the play at the Hadley New Theatre. Ginger, Henry and Douglas (their parents were all going to the opening night, and it had not occurred to any of them to get tickets for the boys) were to spend the evening with William; and Aunt Hester, an aunt of Mr. Brown's who had recently moved to the neighbourhood, was to come over and take charge of them. The parents were to return together at the end of the performance and collect their offspring, after which Mr. Brown was to drive Aunt Hester home. It had seemed an eminently satisfactory arrangement till the news of Hubert and his box and the fact that the play was a harmless thriller had leaked out.

"You may've *ruined* my life," continued William, flinging out his arms again in an impassioned gesture. "I might have turned out a great play-writer if I'd seen that play. It might have given me ideas that'd make me *famous*. Well, if you're goin' to be a great playwriter you've got to see great plays. Stands to reason you have. I bet Shakespeare got that idea of Macbeth with goin' to see a play about a murder an' who did it an' that made him want to have a shot at it himself."

Mrs. Brown laid down her knitting with the air of one tried beyond endurance.

"William," she said, "will you *please* go out and play with someone. I'm tired of the sound of your voice."

William looked at her, amazed and aggrieved.

"Me?" he said. "I've hardly spoke."

But he went out and found Ginger, and the two of them wandered disconsolately through the village towards the old barn. As they passed Hubert Lane's house, Hubert's fat round countenance rose up over the hedge.

"Yah!" he jeered. "Who's got to stay at home next Sat'day! Who's not goin' to see the play at Hadley!"

William gave a scornful but somewhat unconvincing laugh.

"That ole play!" he said. "Gosh! I've got better things to do than seein' that ole play."

"Yah! You'd rather see *Watch with Mother*, wouldn't you?" sneered Hubert. "You wouldn't want to miss Andy Pandy an' the Flowerpot Men, would you?"

"You shut up!" said William fiercely. "They—they're *beggin'* me to go to that ole play an' I may go, after all, or I may stay at home. I've got a lot of important things to do at home jus' now."

Herbert gave a crow of derision.

"Oh, yeah! I know all about that. Auntie's comin' to baby-sit with little Willy, isn't she, while Daddy an' Mummy go out to see the play."

William hurled himself through the garden gate, but Hubert had thoughtfully taken up his position near the entrance to his house so that he could scramble into it in time to slam the door in William's face.

Dejectedly William rejoined Ginger and the two continued their way down the road.

"I scared him all right," said William a little doubtfully. "I jolly well *scared* him."

"He never starts till he's inside his garden near his

138

door," said Ginger. "He'll go on an' on about that play now till it's over. *An'* afterwards."

"Well, I'm jus' about sick of that ole play," said William. "I'm not goin' to think of it again. Ever."

"Yea, let's not," agreed Ginger. "There's lots more int'restin' things in the world than plays. There's that rain gauge we were goin' to make in your garden."

But somehow the rain gauge had lost its interest for them, and their thoughts turned more and more frequently to the play at Hadley New Theatre. Beneath a pretence of indifference they eagerly collected such items of news as trickled through to them. And the items of news were fairly numerous. Sir Roderick Newnham, a well-known London actor, was to be the "guest artist" and take the chief part in the play. Photographs of him—an elegant figure with an imperial beard and smooth, trim moustache—appeared on the front page of the local newspaper, and an interested crowd would generally gather to watch him as he descended from his Jaguar car at the stage door for rehearsals. He did not make himself popular with the inhabitants of Hadley. He referred to Hadley as a "one horse town", called the meals at the Grand Hotel (which advertised "West End Cuisine" and was regarded by its clientele as the height of luxury and sophistication) "pig swill" and compared the bed of ornamental shrubs in Hadley High St, (of which the inhabitants were justly proud), to a "moth eaten bundle of feather dusters".

It turned out, moreover, that Sir Roderick had written his autobiography a couple of years ago and Henry's mother had got the book from the public library.

"I've read bits of it," reported Henry, "an' it's jus' awful. All showin' off. Makin' out he gets the better of every one he meets an' that he's the best actor in the whole world. Makin' out he's been everywhere an' done everythin'. He even said he was made a blood brother by a Red Indian an' given a special blood brother name. I've forgotten what it was. Somethin' like Winnashee or Winnashoo. An' he said he'd shot an elephant"

"Well, that's a jolly cruel thing to do," said William. "Shootin' a poor ole elephant that'd never done him any harm."

"The friend of man," said Henry vaguely.

"An' they're so big he couldn't miss it," said Ginger, "so there's nothin' clever in that."

"He's jus' a rotten ole show-off," said William.

But William's indignation was not really roused against Sir Roderick till he heard about the incident of Robert's motor cycle. The great man, calling at the local garage for petrol and finding his way blocked by Robert's motor cycle, had curtly ordered Robert to take his "toy veteran out of the way and be sharp about it."

This stung William to the quick. Robert's motor cycle was not the latest model and was definitely the worse for wear, but William shared Robert's pride in it and felt that the words were a deadly insult to the whole family.

"Toy veteran!" he said furiously to Ginger. "I wouldn't watch his ole play now, not if he offered me a hundred pounds!"

"Well, he's not likely to," said Ginger, "so you needn't worry about that. . . . Anyway, we said we'd try'n' forget about it."

But it was not so easy to forget about it. Hubert Lane kept up his stream of not very original taunts, adding the Woodentops and Pinky and Perky to his list of the Outlaws' favourite programmes, rising to heights of daring by flinging a ball of mud at Ginger (it missed him) and stretching a piece of string across his garden path to trip up the Outlaws in their pursuit of him and tripping over it himself.

The news that Sir Roderick was going to dinner with the Lanes on the evening of the performance added a fresh spark to the situation. It appeared that Sir Roderick was the friend of a friend of a friend of the Lanes, and

"I know where you'll be," said Hubert.

Mrs. Lane, on discovering this, had tracked him down remorselessly. Hubert became more unbearable than ever as the day drew near.

"Yah!" he shouted. "Think of us on Sat'day havin' Sir Roderick to dinner an' then goin' to see the play in a box."

William gave a snort of amused contempt.

"You'll be jolly surprised when you see where *we* are on Sat'day," he said.

"I know where you'll be," said Hubert. "You'll be bein' tucked into your little cots by Auntie an' havin' a bedtime story read to you."

William's smile was amused and condescending.

"Huh! You wait an' see!" he said. "You're goin' to get a bit of a shock on Sat'day."

The Outlaws passed on down the road. The superior amused smile faded from William's face.

"Why did you say that, William?" said Ginger.

"Jus' to give him somethin' to think of," said William. "He'll be a bit worried now till Sat'day."

"An' worse than ever when it's over," said Douglas gloomily.

"P'raps there'll be such a thick fog that no one can get to the theatre at all," said Ginger.

"Or it might be struck by lightning," said William.

"Or an atomic war might break out," said Henry.

"Or the end of the world might come," said Douglas. "After all, it's got to come sometime."

Cheered by the thought of these possibilities, they walked on briskly down the road.

But the day dawned like any other day and ended uneventfully in a fine mild evening.

Mrs. Brown had provided supper on a lavish scale. There were sausage rolls, sardine sandwiches, doughnuts, jam tarts, cheese straws, chocolate biscuits, fruit salad and raspberry fizz. She had bought several kits for the construction of model cars and aeroplanes and a couple of jigsaw puzzles.

"I'm sure you'll all have a nice evening, dear," she said. "I've taken a lot of trouble over it."

"Thanks," said William.

He tried to infuse the words with scorn, amusement and cynicism . . . and almost succeeded.

"After all, dear," said Mrs. Brown, "you'll have lots more opportunities of going to the New Theatre later on."

"Yes, when I'm an old man," said William bitterly. "I'll be deaf an' blind by the time anyone thinks of takin' *me* to anything."

"Now, William——" began Mrs. Brown, but at this point Ginger, Henry and Douglas arrived. and almost as soon as they had arrived, Mr. Brown rang up to tell Mrs. Brown to catch an earlier bus to Hadley than the one she had arranged to catch.

"The hotel's going to be packed for dinner," he said, "and we shall miss the opening of the play if we don't get going in good time. Catch the earlier bus and I'll meet you at the Hadley bus stop."

Mrs. Brown flew round the house, collecting her belongings.

"Oh, dear!" she said. "How I hate being *rushed* like this! Where are my gloves? What have I done with my handbag? Where are my spectacles?"

The boys stampeded about, finding gloves, handbag and spectacles. Mrs. Brown threw a frantic glance at the clock.

"Oh, dear! Aunt Hester won't be here for another twenty minutes, but you'll be all right, won't you? Don't get into any mischief. . . . There's another tin of chocolate biscuits in the larder and some more jam tarts. . . . Where did I put my keys? Oh, here they are . . . Good-bye and have a nice time."

They accompanied her to the gate, then returned slowly and dejectedly to the house. In spite of the dejection there was a faint undercurrent of excitement at their hearts.

"Food!" said William contemptuously. looking at the

tea-table. "Gosh, they seem to think that food makes up for everythin'." He took up a sausage roll and ate it in three large bits as he continued indistinctly, "They seem to think *food's* all we want. They can go off to plays an' dinner-parties an' think food's all we want. Well," he took up a sardine sandwich and set to work on it, "I jus' don't want to touch their ole food."

"Nor me," said Ginger, making two mouthfuls of a jam tart.

"Nor me," said Henry, demolishing a handful of cheese straws.

Douglas made an indeterminate sound through a doughnut and stretched out his hand for another. Then the telephone bell rang and William, staying only to swallow a glassful of raspberry fizz and half a sausage roll, went into the hall to answer it.

"That you, dear?" said Aunt Hester's voice.

"Yes," said William.

"Well, dear, I want you to give your mother a message from me. I know she won't have started yet but I don't want to drag her to the telephone as I expect she's busy getting ready, but will you tell her that I've got a frightful cold. Quite a sudden one. It came on without warning about half an hour ago while I was feeding the cat. Anyway, I don't want to expose any of you dear boys to infection, so if your mother can make other arrangements —she did say that she could probably arrange for some neighbour to come in if I couldn't manage it—I think I'd be wiser to stay at home. But, if she can't, then of course I'll come along and we'll just trust to providence. Do you understand, dear boy?"

"Uh-huh," said William, guardedly.

"So will you tell her that if she doesn't ring me back within the next ten minutes I'll take for granted that it's all right and that she's been able to find a substitute? Is that quite clear, dear?"

"Yes," said William.

He replaced the receiver and returned to the others.

"Well, you might've left some of the sausage rolls," he said with a disapproving frown.

"Thought you didn't want any of the food," said Ginger.

"No, I don't," said William, making sure of the last sardine sandwich, "an' I wouldn't eat it if they *paid* me for it."

He spoke quite sincerely. His spirit seemed to stand disdainfully aloof while he zestfully assisted his friends to clear the board.

"Well, who was it?" said Ginger at last, wiping a chocolate-circled mouth with the back of his hand.

"It was my aunt that was comin'," said William. He paused a moment before he made the dramatic announcement, "She's not comin'."

They stared at him in silence for a few moments.

"Why?" said Ginger at last.

" 'Cause of a cold she got feedin' the cat."

"You mean," said Henry slowly, "she's not comin' at all?"

"Yes," said William, "she's not comin' at all."

Again they stared at him in silence . . . while the undercurrent of excitement that had been at the bottom of their hearts all evening rose slowly to the surface.

"We can do what we like, then?" said Henry.

"Yes," said William, "we can do what we like."

They went into the sitting-room and looked round at the constructional kits and jigsaw puzzles that Mrs. Brown had so painstakingly provided for them. Comment seemed unnecessary.

"Well, we might as well go out as stay indoors," said William.

"Yes, we might," agreed Ginger.

"It'd do us good to get a breath of fresh air," said Henry.

"Where?" said Douglas.

"That ole Sir Roderick'll be goin' to dinner with the Lanes," said William casually.

"I bet he's not goin' really," said Ginger. "I bet ole Hubert made it up."

"Well, we could go an' *see* if he does," said William.

"I'm not sure we ought to," said Douglas.

But the idea had seized the imagination of the others.

"Come on," said William, turning to the door. There he stopped and added, "There's nothin' *wrong* in jus' goin' for a little walk to get a breath of fresh air. That's all it is. Jus' a quiet little walk to get a breath of fresh air . . . an' prob'ly jus' happen to go past Hubert's house . . . jus' to see if this ole Sir Roderick's *axshully* gone there."

Gleefully they sallied forth, walking quickly down the lane that led to Hubert's house. Excitement rose higher in them, they couldn't have told why . . . then they stood for some minutes in the gathering dusk watching the closed front door. There was no sign of hosts or guests.

"No good stayin' here," said William at last. "If he does come he'll jus' drive up in that awful car of his an' go straight into the house. We'd have no time even to speak to him. We couldn't *do* anythin'. Let's walk on a bit. We don't want him to think we're waitin' to see him. Gosh! He's conceited enough without that. Come on."

They walked on slowly down the road. William broke the silence.

"Let's have a sort of game," he said. "Fixin' up what

146

we'd have done if we *had* met him, if we'd met him walking along an' not sure where Hubert's house was."

"Well, what would we have done?" said Ginger.

"Kidnapped him," said Douglas, "so he couldn't act in that play."

"It's not so easy kidnappin' people," said Henry. "You've got to have somewhere to take them to an' keep them there an' we haven't got anywhere."

"The old barn," suggested Ginger.

"Yes, an' how'd we *get* him there an' how'd we *keep* him there? You can't even shut the door prop'ly. It'd be a jolly funny sort of kidnappin'."

"There mus' be other places," said Ginger.

"Yes, let's think," said William.

The idea was taking hold of them. They had almost forgotten the imaginary nature of the situation. It had become real, urgent.

"There's your coal shed," said Ginger.

"Yes, an' how'd we keep him in it?" said Henry. "He'd shout the place down, too, an' get let out an' we'd be the ones in trouble, not him."

"*Tell* you what!" said William. He stopped short in his tracks. "I've got an idea."

They gathered round him in respectful silence.

"The old quarry on the Marleigh road," he said.

"How d'you mean?" said Ginger.

"Well, if we got him down there, he'd never get up. Not 'less we showed him the secret way we get up. An' no one'd hear him shoutin' down there."

"Yes, an' how're we goin' to get him down?" said Ginger.

"We can't push him down," said Douglas. "There's laws against it. There's the Magna Carta."

They began to walk slowly along the road again.

147

"Anyway we *couldn't* push him down," said Henry. "He'd be more likely to push us down."

"*Tell* you what!" said William, stopping short in his tracks again.

Again they gathered round him.

"Those Red Indians. . . . The ones in his book. . . ."

"Well?" said Ginger.

"Well, he said he'd been made the blood brother of one an' given a blood brother name an' I once read a story about that an' if one of them's in danger an calls out the name of the other then he's *got* to go to the rescue. If he doesn't, curses follow him for the rest of his life. What was the name, Henry?"

"I don't remember very well," said Henry. "Somethin' like Wannashee or Wannshoo. . . ."

"Well," said William, "if one of us called his blood brother name out of the quarry, he'd have to go down to help. He'd be a man under a curse for the rest of his life if he didn't. He'd *have* to."

"An' then what'll happen?" said Douglas. "We can't leave him to starve to death in a quarry. There's laws against that, too."

"Oh, no," said William, "we'll keep him there jus' till the play's over so's he can't go to dinner with ole Hubert or act in the play. It'll serve him right for calling Robert's motor cycle a 'toy veteran' an' it'll serve my family right for not takin' me"

"I 'spect he's got an understudy," said Henry.

"Yes," said William, "but I heard Robert say that his understudy's got an awful cold an' can't say a word without sneezin', so it'd jolly well serve *everyone* right. An', when it's nearly the time the play finishes an' it's too late for him to act in it, we'll tell him the way we get up out of the quarry."

148

"We'll get into the biggest row we've ever got into in the whole of our lives," said Douglas.

"It'll have been worth it," said William grimly. "We'll have *shown* 'em all—him an' Hubert *an* our fam'lies. . . . Oh, well. . . ." He shrugged his shoulders and continued flatly, "It was only a sort of make-up game. Waste of time, too, when we might have been doin' somethin' int'restin'."

"Funny that we're goin' along the Marleigh road," said Ginger thoughtfully, "an' that we've nearly got to the old quarry."

"Yes," said William, "I hadn't noticed but"—he gave his short sarcastic laugh—"we're not likely to find him wanderin' alone on the Marleigh road miles away from Hadley an' the theatre an' Hubert's house "

"There's someone comin' along behind us," said Ginger, sinking his voice to a whisper.

They slackened their pace and listened. Footsteps sounded behind them, coming nearer. . . .

They turned, then stood, open-mouthed with amazement. There was no mistaking the tall elegant figure, the imperial beard, the smooth trim moustache.

"Gosh!" said William faintly.

"Good evening," said the man and made as if to pass them, but William took his position on one side and Henry on the other, with Ginger and Douglas behind. The five walked on together down the road. The man ignored his companions.

"Nice evening," said Henry tentatively.

The man made no response.

"Er—you goin' to the Lanes'?" said William.

The man remained silent.

"But cold for the time of the year," said Henry.

Still the man made no response.

149

"You'll prob'ly get to the Lanes' if you go straight on," said William, encouragingly.

The man still ignored them.

"It's an int'restin' bit of country," said Henry.

"There's an old church built in—in the Bronze Age," said William, "an' a statue of a man that went to the crusades with his legs crossed.

Suddenly a cry rang out through the air.

"Winna-*shoo!*"

William turned round. Ginger was no longer there. The cry rang out again.

"Winna-*shoo!*"

Then, without a moment's hesitation, the man darted to the low railings that separated the road from the quarry, flung himself over the edge and disappeared.

"Gosh!" said William again.

"Ginger went down," explained Douglas. "He knew the man wouldn't notice him goin' so he went down an' did the blood brother cry."

"Then he *was* a blood brother," said William. "P'raps we misjudged him."

"He won't misjudge us," said Henry, "when he comes up . . . if he ever does come up."

They craned their necks over the railing, peering into the dusk-shrouded quarry and were rewarded at last by the sight of Ginger scrambling up behind a shrub that grew sheer from the cliff.

"You clot, Ginger!" said William. "I didn't mean you axshully to *do* it."

"I know," said Ginger apologetically. "I'm sorry. . . . It jus' came over me suddenly, seein' him an' the quarry there together. It made it all seem *real*."

"Well, you've made it real all right," said William. "He prob'ly won't get to the play at all now. . . ." He

"Nice evening," said Henry tentatively The man male
no response. "Er—you goin' to the Lanes'?" said William.
The man remained silent.

stopped and listened. No sound came from the quarry. "You'd think he'd be shoutin' for help or somethin'. He mus' have found that there's no one there. I wonder what he's doin'."

"Prob'ly starvin' to death," said Douglas gloomily, "an' they'll say it's our fault. They always do."

They listened again. There was still no sound from below.

"I hope he's not broken his neck," said Henry.

"Or bashed his head open on a stone," said Ginger.

"He sounds dead to me," said Douglas.

Again they listened. Again only silence answered them.

"Let's shout," said Henry. "Let's shout 'Hi!' an' see if he answers."

They shouted "Hi" with all the strength of their young lungs. The echoes died away and were followed again by silence.

"You'd think we'd hear him moanin' an' groanin' if he's bashed his head open," said Henry. "I wonder if we ought to fetch the police."

"Why?" said William.

"It might be our duty as citizens."

"It's a bit late to think of that," said William. "It wasn't our duty as citizens to push him down a quarry."

"We didn't push him," said Douglas.

"We *lured* him," said Ginger, "an' I did it jolly well."

"Let's listen again," said William.

They listened again . . . and this time they heard faint scrambling sounds, sounds that grew nearer and louder . . . till suddenly the familiar imperial beard and smooth trim moustache emerged from one of the bushes near the top, and the man pulled himself up and stepped lightly through the railings to join the boys on the road.

"Hello!" he said casually. "You still here?"

He was a deplorable sight. His hair was dishevelled, his face smeared and scratched, his coat and jacket torn, his shoes mud-covered.

"We—we're sorry," said William, "we didn't mean. . . . It was a sort of game an' it suddenly went real."

Suddenly the familiar imperial beard and trim moustache emerged . . .

The man's whole attention seemed to be given to brushing bits of mud and cliff-face from his thousers.

"How did you get up?" said Ginger. "We thought there was only our way."

"Oh, I'm a pretty sound mountaineer" said the man. "I've done quite a bit over the Alps and the Dolomites."

He perched on the railings and began to wipe the mud off his shoes with handfuls of grass.

"We're sorry," said William again. "We didn't mean to get you all messed up like this jus' when you've got to act in the play."

"I'm not acting in the play," said the man.

They stared at him.

"You—you are Sir Roderick Newnham, aren't you?" said William.

"Oh, no," said the man. "I'm not unlike him, of course. We're often mistaken for each other. We wear the same sort of whiskers. We wore them before we met each other, and I didn't see why I should give them up just because he wore them, and he didn't seen why he should give them up just because I wore them."

"Oh," said William.

The situation seemed to be getting beyond him.

"Well, if you've nothin' to do with the play——" he began.

"Oh, but I have," said the man, "but while Sir Roderick's at the top I'm at the bottom. I'm the least important person in it. The lowest of the low."

"The call-boy?" suggested Henry.

"Much less important than that. I'm the author of the book from which the play was adapted. You can't get lower than that." He spoke quite cheerfully. "You won't know my name—it's printed on the poster in such small letters that no one can read it—but it's Guy Boscastle."

"Oh," said William again.

"Then you aren't any Red Indian's blood brother?" said Ginger.

"Not that I know of," said Mr. Boscastle, removing some stones from his collar.

"Well, when I called 'Winnashoo' from the quarry——"

"Oh, was that what the yell was?" said Mr. Boscastle. I thought I heard the sound of someone falling into water——"

"It was me," said Ginger. "I didn't fall into that pool at the bottom of the quarry, but the piece of rock I was holdin' on to did."

"Then I heard this cry for help——"

"It was your blood brother's name," said Ginger.

"Oh," said Mr. Boscastle. "I didn't realise that, of course. I plunged down to the rescue and found no one there so thought it might have been some sort of bird-note. I'm not very well up in birds. But what's all this about, anyway?"

Disjointedly and a little incoherently they explained the situation. Mr. Boscastle listened with grunts of understanding and occasional interruptions.

"Not a bad chap really, old Roddy. A bit cantankerous, like most V.I.P.'s, but not a bad chap really. . . . Yes, he said he'd been asked to dinner by some people—I'm afraid he called them 'wretched natives'—but didn't intend to go."

"You stayed down there a long time," said Ginger.

"Yes, the place gave me the most marvellous idea. Come and sit down and I'll tell you all about it." They took their seats beside him on the railing. "You see, I'm hard at work on another book. It's a thriller, of course, and I'd meant to have a chase in the last chapter. You know the sort of thing. Villain and hero pursuing each other for page after page. Dodging, hiding, grappling, ambushing each other, dashing after each other. Hero nearly killed twenty times over but saved by a sort of miracle each time and, of course, coming out on top in the end."

"They generally do," said Henry with a touch of cynicism in his voice.

"Where were they goin' to have the chase?" said William.

"That's the whole point," said Mr. Boscastle. "I'd thought of one of the disused stations—overgrown by weeds and infested by rats. It seemed a grand idea at first —dodging in and out of the ruined waiting-room and ticket-office, scrambling in and out of the broken windows of the refreshment room, but, when I came to tackle it, it fell absolutely flat. The whole thing was on too small a scale. It gave one no scope . . . and, of course, there was nothing to stop either of them just sloping off down the permanent way when he'd had enough."

"So what did you do?" said William.

"I came out for a walk to try and think out another idea. . . ."

"Was that why you didn't answer when we spoke to you?"

"Probably. I'm apt to be a bit absent-minded when I'm trying to think something out. . . Anyway, when I got to the bottom of the quarry and looked about me— well, it seemed to hit me in the eyes. It was the ideal place for a chase. There are caves, rocks, boulders, thick bushes growing up the sides, that gloomy-looking pool at the bottom."

"We once sailed a raft on it," said William.

"We didn't get far," said Henry.

"Anyway, I saw at once that it was the ideal place for the chase. They could ambush each other, hurl boulders on each other, hide from each other, drop down on each other . . ."

"Push each other into the pond," said William.

"Fasten each other up in caves," said Ginger.

156

Hubert Lane's mouth dropped open.

"Fall from dizzy heights," said Douglas.

"Yes, all that," said Mr. Boscastle. "The possibilities are endless. The thing can be crammed with tension and adventure and suspense. And, of course, the quarry would be a sort of trap. Neither of them could escape."

"And was that why you were so long down there?" said Henry.

"Yes, I was visualising the whole thing. I was memorising every detail. Suddenly it all became *alive* as I looked at it." He jumped to his feet. "In fact I can't wait to get going on it. It's bubbling up in my head like a geyser. I'm almost writing it as I stand here. In an hour I shall be well away with it."

"But—aren't you goin' to see your play?" said William.

"No," said Mr. Boscastle. "They've kindly put a box at my disposal, but I didn't really want to see it in any case. I shouldn't recognise a single word. They've mauled it to death." He spoke without resentment. "I'm not blaming them. They can't help it. It's their nature. No, I I shall go straight to my desk and start on the quarry chapter. It's going to be *grand*." He looked at them as if struck by a sudden idea. "I suppose you wouldn't care to use the box by any chance?"

They gasped and gaped.

"You don't mean—you're givin' it to us—your box?" said William.

"Certainly, if you'd like to use it. It's little enough return for what you've done for me. You've *made* my last chapter. You've saved my book."

William, Ginger, Henry and Douglas entered the box and took their seats in decorous silence It was the stage box—the best box in the house. Turning to survey his surroundings, William met the gaze of Hubert Lane who, with his parents, occupied the next box—a vastly inferior affair, its view of the stage impeded by the box that the Outlaws occupied. Hubert's mouth dropped open, his face turned green with rage and anguish. William flashed at him a grimace expressive of triumph, amusement and contempt. Hubert had a pretty good grimace of his own, but he was past using it.

The lights were going down. William, glancing at the stalls, saw his parents' faces upraised to him, frozen into masks of incredulous amazement.

He threw them a smile of distant and dignified recognition, raised a hand in careless greeting, then turned his whole attention to the stage.